NICK FURY™ VS. S.H.I.E.L.D.™

chapter one: *THE DELTA EQUATION*

TOPSIDE TO COLONEL FURY ¬SQUARWK¬ TOPSIDE...DO YOU BRZZZT *COPY*? REPORT STATUSSSS

I HEAR YA, *GAFF*, BUT NONE TOO CLEAR.

WE CAN BARELY *READ YOU*, NICK, IT'S WHAT I WAS AFRAID OF. THE *POWER CORE* COULD BE INTERFERING WITH YOUR SIGNAL. HAVE YOU *REACHED* IT YET?

NEGATIVE... ¬SQUARWK¬... CENTRAL SHAFT...IS TAKIN' LONGER...HMMMM... WE THOUGHT...

BE CAREFUL, *NICKIE*, IT'S VERY *UNSTABLE* IN THERE. I SWEAR THAT YOU'RE GONNA GIVE ME A *HEART ATTACK* ONE DAY. WE GOT *SHIELD'S* BEST RECOVERY TEAM HERE, AND YOU *INSIST* ON GOIN' DOWN *ALONE*!

NICK, *CLAY QUARTERMAIN* AND HIS MEN ARE READY TO GO DOWN AT A MOMENT'S NOTICE!

FORGET IT, *GAFFER!* YOU KNOW NICK ISN'T ABOUT TO LET *US* RISK OUR NECKS WHILE HE SITS ON HIS DUFF TOPSIDE. HE'S GOT TO BE WHERE THE *ACTION IS*.

FURY TO TOPSIDE. MY METER IS PICKIN' UP READIN'S. THE CORE IS DEFINITELY *HOT!* I'M MOVIN' ON...

BEEP BEEP BEEP BEEP

SO THE PRELIMINARY REPORTS WERE *RIGHT*. THE CORE'S BEEN *ACTIVATED*. GAFF, YOU'RE OUR RESIDENT *GENIUS*, HOW'S IT *POSSIBLE?*

YA GOT ME, *CLAY*, BUT RIGHT NOW I DON'T GIVE A FLYING *FIG* FOR THE WHYS AND WHEREFORES.

ALL I CARE ABOUT IS THAT WE'RE SITTIN' ON TOP OF THE BIGGEST DESTRUCTIVE DEVICE SINCE THE *H-BOMB*.

AND IT AIN'T EXACTLY A *NICE FEELIN'*.

CAN'T SEE A *THING*, COMMANDER... EXCEPT THAT A LOT OF DEBRIS GOT CARRIED DOWN IN THE COLLAPSE. THE SHAFT IS ACTUALLY *WIDER*.

QUARTERMAIN TO FURY! QUARTERMAIN TO FURY! CAN YOU HEAR ME? *ANSWER ME*, NICK!

ANSWER ME, BLAST IT!

FURY HERE, CLAY. JUST NEEDED A SECOND TO CATCH MY *BREATH*. THIS STUFF USED TO BE FUN, BUT I THINK I'M GETTIN' TOO OLD FOR IT.

TELL THE GAFFER I WANT A MEETIN' WITH THE JOKER WHO DECIDED THIS WAS THE *SAFEST ENTRY POINT.* IS EVERYONE ALL RIGHT UP THERE?

EVERYONE'S FINE, NICK. GIVE US HALF AN HOUR. WE'RE COMING DOWN TO *HELP* YOU.

NEGATIVE, TOPSIDE. *NO ONE* COMES DOWN TILL I MARK OFF A COURSE TO THE CORE, *GOT IT?* THE WRECK'S TOO DANGEROUS.

YOU'RE THE BOSS.

SOME TIME LATER, AT THE BOTTOM OF THE SHAFT...

SCANNER SAYS I CAN'T BE TOO FAR AWAY. BEEPER AGREES, BUT I DON'T RECOGNIZE A *THING* IN THIS MESS...

BABE, THEY REALLY DID A *JOB* ON YOU.

BEEP
BEEP
BEEP
BEEP

"YOU WERE *SHIELD'S* PROUDEST BIT OF EQUIPMENT, OUR FLAGSHIP, THE *HELICARRIER,* A FLYIN' FORTRESS THAT ENABLED US TO BE MOBILE IN A MOMENT'S NOTICE...

"...UNTIL YOU *CRASHED* MONTHS AGO HERE IN THE DESERT. THE BOARD AIN'T AUTHORIZED THE FUNDS FOR A REPLACEMENT. THEY WEREN'T TOO HAPPY THAT THE CRASH WAS CAUSED BY A RENEGADE *SHIELD* AGENT.

"NOT THAT I *BLAME* 'EM...IT WOULD BE ONE THING IF THE CARRIER HAD GONE DOWN DEFENDIN' THE COUNTRY AGAINST *HYDRA* OR *AIM* OR ANY OTHER GOON SQUAD *SHIELD* WAS CREATED TO BATTLE...

...BUT WE DID IT TO *OURSELVES.* SOMETHIN' JUST AIN'T RIGHT ANY MORE. THE LAST FEW YEARS THERE'S BEEN SO MANY MISHAPS... AGENTS STEPPIN' OUTTA LINE-- SOMETIMES I THINK I OUGHTA PACK IT--

WELL, KISS MY NOSE!

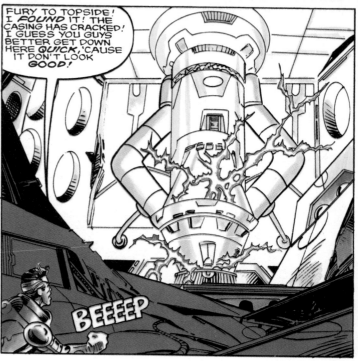

FURY TO TOPSIDE! I *FOUND* IT! THE CASING HAS CRACKED! I GUESS YOU GUYS BETTER GET DOWN HERE *QUICK,* 'CAUSE IT DON'T LOOK *GOOD!*

BEEEEP

SOME TWO HOURS LATER...

IT'S REALLY *FLARIN'* NOW, NICKIE.

THANKS, GAFF, I NEVER WOULDA *NOTICED*. YOU SURE IT'S SAFE FOR *CLAY* AND THE *SALVAGE CREW* TO GET SO BLAMED CLOSE?

SURE. THEY'RE BEHIND AN ADAMANTIUM-BASED POLYMER *SAFETY SCREEN*. NOTHING'LL GET THROUGH THAT BABY... EXCEPT OF COURSE WHEN THE CORE REACHES *CRITICAL*. NOTHIN' WILL SAVE YOU FROM THAT!

YOU'RE A REAL *OPTIMIST*, YOU KNOW THAT, GAFF? WE GOTTA MOVE THE CORE TO THE *BAFFLE CUBE* FAST!

WHEN WE CAN, WE WILL, NICK. I STILL DON'T KNOW *HOW* THIS HAPPENED. I MADE THE FIRST SCAN OF THE WRECK. OUR ROBOT MONITORS SHOWED THAT THE CORE WAS ENTIRELY *INTACT*. THE *CRASH* DID NOT DAMAGE THE CASING. SOMEONE HAD TO DO IT *AFTERWARDS*.

THAT AIN'T POSSIBLE. THE WRECK HAS BEEN UNDER *CONSTANT SURVEILLANCE*. WE GOT AN ENTIRE *SQUAD* STATIONED HERE. NOBODY GETS WITHIN *THIRTY MILES* OF THIS PLACE WITHOUT ME KNOWIN' ABOUT IT.

WHATEVER, NICKIE. THE THING THAT MATTERS IS THAT THE CORE'S BEEN RELEASED FROM ITS *BAFFLE-CASING*... ONCE VIOLATED, THE SAFETY SYSTEMS *FAIL*, AND THE CORE GOES *CRITICAL*.

YEAH, WELL I NEVER LIKED FLYIN' IN A TUB THAT WAS POWERED BY SOMETHIN' THAT COULD *VAPORIZE* YOU IN A SECOND.

NICK, GAFF...

THE PRELIMINARY SCANS ARE FINISHED. WE'VE GOT ABOUT AN *HOUR* TO MOVE THE CORE TO THE NEW RESTRAINING CUBE... IF WE DON'T *NEW MEXICO* BECOMES ONE BIG *HOLE* ON THE MAP.

GREAT.

COLONEL FURY, WE'VE FOUND SOMETHING!

WHAT NOW--?

WE DISCOVERED THEM ON OUR *FINAL SCAN*. YOU'LL NEED YOUR *PROTECTIVE BINOCULARS*, SIR.

WELL, GAFF, LOOKS LIKE I OWE YOU AN *APOLOGY*...

"WE GOT US TWO DEAD MEN OUT THERE. MUSTA DIED THE SECOND THEY CRACKED THE *CASING*. HOW DID THEY GET *IN* HERE? WHO--?"

DEAR HEAVEN! NICK, IT'S A *POWER SURGE!*

CCRRRACKK

KA-BLOOM

EVERYONE GET BACK!

GAFFER! WHAT HAPPENED? WHAT'S GOIN' ON?

FZZZZZZZZZZ

GOOD LORD! THE SAFETY DEVICES MUST HAVE BEEN DAMAGED FAR *WORSE* THAN WE THOUGHT! THE POWER CYLINDER'S BEEN EXPOSED AND IT'S GOING *HAYWIRE!*

THE *RAO-* LEVELS ARE GOING OFF THE SCALE! WHAT DO WE DO NOW?

DO? WE PRAY, CLAY BOY, WE PRAY! THE CORE IS COLLECTING ALL THE RANDOM ENERGIES IN THIS CHAMBER, ABSORBING THEM AND USING THEM TO BUILD TO CRITICAL MASS! AND WHEN IT DOES--

--A WHOLE CHUNK OF REAL ESTATE IS GONNA BE HISTORY!

NOT IF *I* CAN HELP IT, GAFFER-- AND I GUESS I GOTTA *TRY.*

NICK, NO! ARE YOU INSANE? YOU SAW WHAT IT DID TO THOSE MEN! LET ME CALL IN *REINFORCEMENTS!*

THERE AIN'T NO TIME, QUARTERMAIN! NOW LEGGO! THAT'S AN ORDER!

NICK!

I WISH I KNEW WHAT I WUZ PLANNIN' TO *DO* WITH THIS THING. BUT I JUST CAN'T STAND BY AND DO *NOTHIN'.*

FSSSSSSSS

WHOA! THIS THING IS HOT... AND IT'S PRODUCIN' SOME SORT OF *ENERGY FIELD*... PUSHIN' ME BACK... BUT I GOTTA FIGHT IT...

GOT IT! NOW TO MOVE IT *OUTTA* HERE... BUT... *NUTS*... MY SUIT... IT'S MELTIN'...!

THE LIGHT IS SO INTENSE... CAN BARELY SEE A THING...

GOTTA CARRY IT... BUT MY LEGS GONE ALL RUBBERY ON ME... DON'T FEEL 'EM...

C'MON, FURY! *MOVE!* BLAST IT, YOU LIVED THROUGH THREE WARS... YOU AIN'T GONNA BE BEAT BY SOME *RIDICULOUS GLOWIN' GARBAGE CAN!*

WHO AM I KIDDIN'? IT'S NO GOOD... I... CAN'T... MAKE... IT... ALL THOSE PEOPLE... I...

WHA--? LIFTING?

C'MON, BOSS, I'M NOT LETTING YOU GRAB *ALL* THE GLORY.

CLAY?

LET'S GET THIS BABY OUT OF HERE!

HURRY! THE FURTHER WE GET THIS CORE FROM THIS ENERGY CHAMBER, THE *BETTER!*

DID ANYONE EVER TELL THE TWO OF YOU THAT YOU HAVE A HECKUVA LOT OF *CHUTZPAH?* SHEESH!

NOW, C'MON, WE GOTTA GET THE CORE OVER TO THIS ENERGY DAMPER!

GET OUT TO THE CONTAINMENT CUBE AS FAST AS POSSIBLE! WE'RE NOT EXACTLY OUTTA DANGER YET, Y'KNOW.

THE DAMPER WON'T BE ABLE TO CONTAIN THE THE CORE FOR LONG-- WE MAY ONLY HAVE DELAYED OUR DEATHS FOR A MINUTE.

SOMEONE REMIND ME NOT TO TAKE THE GAFF ON ANY MORE FIELD TRIPS... HE'S SUCH A JOY TO HAVE AROUND.

AND WITHIN MINUTES, THE CORE IS TRANSPORTED TO A SPECIALLY PREPARED SITE...

ALL PERSONNEL! ALERT! THE CORE IS REACHING CRITICAL MASS! ALERT!

ARROGAH

C'MON, CLAY, LET'S GET THIS CONTRAPTION IN THE CONTAINER SO WE CAN SHUT THAT BLASTED ALARM OFF!

ARROGAH

NICE AND EASY... THIS OVERSIZED BUILDING BLOCK IS SUPPOSE TO NEUTRALIZE THE CORE...LET'S HOPE IT DOES IT!

ARRO

OKAY... IT'S IN, LET'S HOPE WE WERE IN TIME...

ARROOGAHH

CORE READINGS RETURNING TO NORMAL. CONTAINMENT INTERLOCKS ARE ACHIEVING BALANCE.

CRISIS IS PASSED.

GOOD JOB, CLAY--THANKS.

LATER, IN THE DECONTAMINATION CHAMBER...

C'MON, GAFF, HOW MUCH LONGER WE GOTTA *FLOAT* IN THIS OVERGROWN BATHTUB? IT'S BEEN *FOUR HOURS!*

CALM DOWN, NICKIE. YOU AND CLAY WERE EXPOSED TO THE HIGHEST RAD LEVELS. SO YOU GOTTA TAKE A LITTLE *LONGER SWIM.* ENJOY IT! THINK OF IT AS A BUBBLE BATH.

JUST BE GRATEFUL THE CORE IS SECURE. I KNOW *I'M* GONNA SLEEP TONIGHT...

ALL RIGHT, LET'S CUT THE CRAP... HOW MANY DID WE *LOSE?*

SIX ON THE RECOVERY TEAM DIED IN THE FLARE-UP OR RIGHT AFTERWARDS... I WASN'T GONNA TELL YOU UNTIL AFTER DECOM WAS COMPLETE.

ALSO, THE TWO DEAD INTRUDERS WERE *VAPORIZED.* NO WAY NOW WE CAN TELL WHO THEY *WERE.*

BUT WE'RE *GOIN' TO,* GAFF. WE *HAVE* TO. SOMEHOW TWO MEN VIOLATED A SHIELD SECURITY AREA WITHOUT BEING DETECTED... UNLEASHED A DEADLY POWER SOURCE AND NEARLY DESTROYED A LARGE CHUNK OF REAL ESTATE. YOU CAN *BET* WE'RE GONNA FIND OUT WHO THEY WERE!

SOMEWHERE ELSE...

THE POWER CORE HAS BEEN RECOVERED.

YOU *ARE* AWARE THAT NICHOLAS IS THERE?

VERY GOOD. PROCEED WITH THE NEXT STEP.

OF COURSE. THE DIVERSION WILL ENTERTAIN HIM.

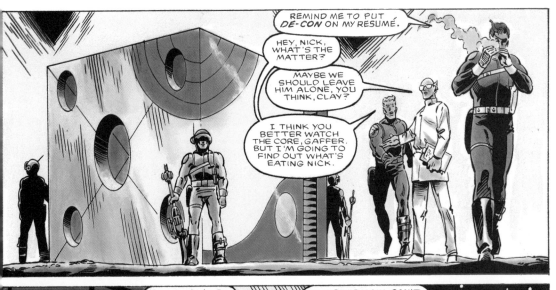

REMIND ME TO PUT *DE-CON* ON MY *RESUME.*

HEY, NICK, WHAT'S THE MATTER?

MAYBE WE SHOULD LEAVE HIM ALONE, YOU THINK, CLAY?

I THINK YOU BETTER WATCH THE CORE, GAFFER. BUT I'M GOING TO FIND OUT WHAT'S EATING NICK.

COLONEL! HEY, NICK, WAIT UP!

QUARTERMAIN, CAN'T A MAN SMOKE HIS CIGAR IN PEACE AROUND HERE?

COME ON, NICK. SPILL IT. WHAT'S WRONG?

WRONG? NOTHIN' 'CEPT FOR THE FACT THAT *SHIELD* WAS ALMOST RESPONSIBLE FOR WIPIN' OUT MILLIONS OF LIVES TODAY. EVERYTHING'S PERFECT. IT AIN'T SUPPOSED TO WORK LIKE THIS. WE'RE SUPPOSED TO *PROTECT* PEOPLE... MAKE THE WORLD A BETTER PLACE.

LEAST THAT'S WHAT I THOUGHT. INSTEAD, WE GO AROUND PLAYIN' PATTY CAKE WITH THINGS THAT CAN END IT ALL. I DUNNO. MAYBE OUR TOYS ARE JUST TOO BIG FOR US.

NICK, YOU KNOW WE HAVE A *JOB* TO DO, AND IT'S NOT AN EASY ONE. IT'S MORE THAN THAT, ISN'T IT?

Y'KNOW, I NEVER LIKED FEELIN' SORRY FOR MYSELF. IT'S A WASTE OF TIME. BUT THERE AIN'T NO USE DENYIN' THE FACT THAT I COULDN'T *CUT IT* TODAY. IF IT WASN'T FOR *YOU,* THAT CORE WOULD HAVE GONE *CRITICAL...*

AW, WHO AM I KIDDIN'? I'M GETTIN' TOO *OLD* FOR THIS HIGH TECH CLOAK AND DAGGER BUSINESS. MEBBE I'M JUST AN OLD DOG SOLDIER WHO GOT IN WAY OVER HIS HEAD. MEBBE I'M JUST--

NICK, *LOOK!*

WHA--

AN A.I.M. SHIP! LOOKS LIKE *THIS* OLD MAN AIN'T GETTIN' ANY REST TONIGHT! LET'S MOVE!

IT'S HUGE! HOW DID IT GET PAST OUR SCANNERS?

"COLONEL! THOSE ARE *HYDRA* AGENTS FLYING OUT OF THAT SHIP!

"I STILL GOT *ONE* GOOD EYE, QUARTERMAIN. LOOKS LIKE OUR BUDDIES ARE GOING FOR *BROKE* ON THIS ONE. THIS IS A *FULL-SCALE ATTACK!*"

AAAGH

FZWAT

RUNCITER!

YOU *ARE* A PRETTY ONE. IT IS A PITY MY ORDERS ARE EXPLICIT-- *NO SURVIVORS!*

I'M TOO FAR AWAY. I'LL NEVER *REACH* HER IN TIME!

THIS BABY OUGHTA DO THE TRICK!

ONE MULTI-MAGNESIUM FLARE PELLET COMIN' UP!

ZZZ

WHA--?

NNNN

AAAH! THAT LIGHT!

FFZZZATT

OUT O' MY WAY, CHARLIE!

COLONEL!

ACK

CHUMP

FFWAT

YOU OKAY, RUNCITER?

YES, I -- COLONEL, LOOK!

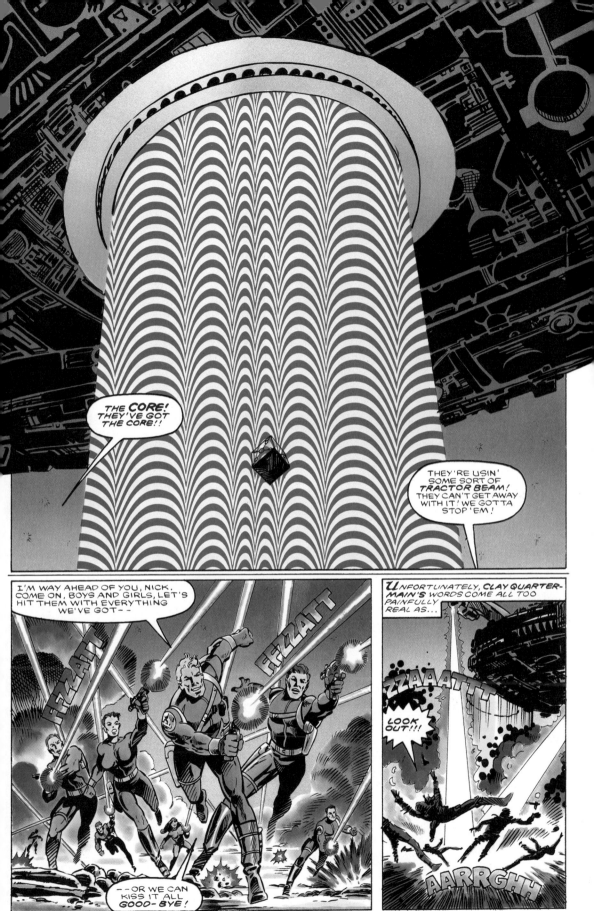

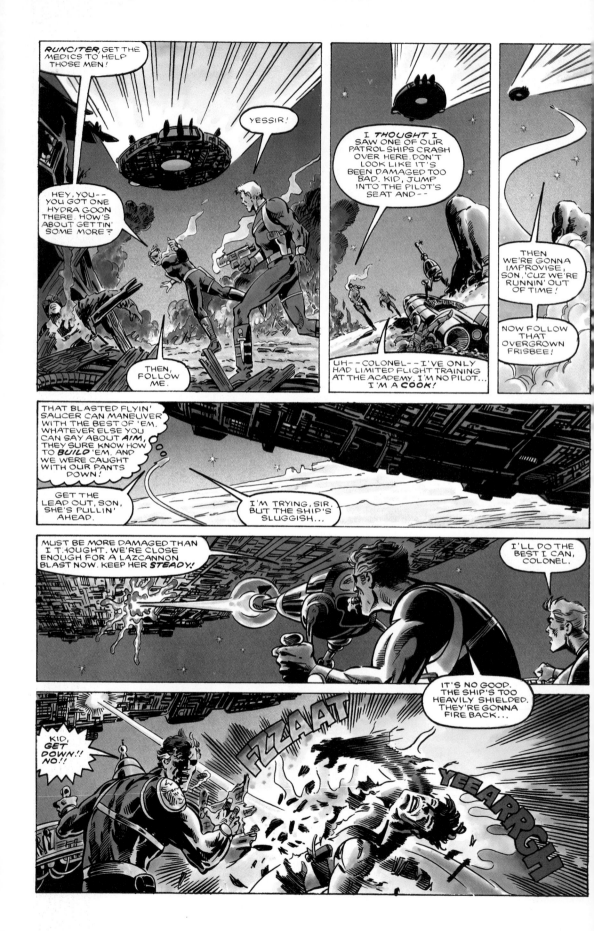

FREED NOW FROM PURSUIT, THE *AIM* STEALTH CRAFT SOARS INTO THE NIGHT SKY...

KID, ARE YOU ALL RIGHT? *ANSWER ME!* BLAST IT!

AWW, NO... HE'S *GONE.* DON'T WORRY, SON, WE'LL GET THOSE SLIME, WE'LL MAKE 'EM PAY.

...AS THE HEAVILY DAMAGED *SHIELD* PATROL CRAFT PLUMMETS TO EARTH.

NICE PROMISE, FURY. NICE EMPTY WORDS THAT AIN'T GONNA DO *HIM* ANY GOOD.

AND *YOUR* NUMBER'S GONNA BE UP IF YOU DON'T BRING THIS TUB *DOWN.* THE CONTROL CONSOLE'S BEEN BLOWN TO BITS, BUT MAYBE I CAN JIMMY SOMETHIN' TOGETHER...

GOTTA CLEAR THAT SAND DUNE!

THUUMPF SCREEEE

PUN-CRASH

WELL, FURY, YOU MADE IT ONE MORE TIME. HOORAY. THE GOOD GUYS *ALWAYS* COME OUT ON TOP. YEAH. TELL THAT TO MY MEN BACK THERE WHO DIDN'T MAKE IT. TELL THAT TO ALL THOSE PEOPLE WHO DEPEND ON US--ON ME--TO *PROTECT* 'EM. NOW *AIM'S* GOT THE POWER CORE AND THERE WASN'T A THING I COULD DO.

LATER, AS THE MEDIVAC TEAMS ARRIVE TO SEE TO THE INJURED...

NICK! I'VE BEEN LOOKING ALL OVER FOR YOU! WHAT ARE WE GONNA DO? THEY'VE GOT THE CORE, NICK! IT'S BAD--IT'S VERY, VERY BAD!

DO YOU THINK I'M AN IDIOT, LEVINE? I KNOW IT'S BAD!

NOW, GET OUTTA MY WAY, THAT'S CLAY, OVER THERE.

H--HEY, N-NICK... WHY THE L-LONG FACE? C'MON, DON'T TAKE IT SO H-HARD...

HOW ELSE AM I SUPPOSED TO TAKE IT, CLAY? NOW JUST BE QUIET...AND CONCENTRATE ON GETTIN' BETTER. SHIELD NEEDS YOU, PAL!

HE DOESN'T LOOK GOOD, GAFF. THIS WHOLE BLAMED RECOVERY OPERATION HAS BLOWN UP IN OUR FACES. AND I'M SICK OF IT! I'M SICK OF WATCHIN' GOOD MEN AND WOMEN DIE. I'M SICK OF FIGHTIN' A WAR I CAN'T WIN. WHAT'S THE POINT OF IT ALL, EH, GAFF? CAN YOU TELL ME THAT?

NICKY, I'M SORRY I SNAPPED AT YOU BEFORE. IT'S JUST THAT...

IT'S JUST THAT ONE OF THE MOST EVIL ORGANIZATION KNOWN TO MAN HAS JUST STOLEN ONE OF THE MOST POWERFUL ENERGY SOURCES ON EARTH. HECK, IF YOU CAN'T GET TESTY NOW, WHEN CAN YOU?

COLONEL FURY, A MESSAGE...

NOT NOW, RUNCITER.

THE TRANSMISSION IS OVER YOUR PRIVATE FREQUENCY, COLONEL PRIORITY 1A.

AND I HAVE STANDING ORDERS TO RELAY ANY AND ALL 1A TRANSMISSIONS TO THE DIRECTOR IMMEDIATELY...

PLEASE, RUNCITER! YA DON'T HAVE TO READ ME THE RULE BOOK, I PRACTICALLY WROTE THE BLAMED THING. LET ME HEAR.

IT'S IN YOUR PRIVATE CODE, SIR. ONLY YOU CAN DECODE IT.

SEVERAL SECONDS LATER...

RUNCITER, GET ME A SHUTTLE CRAFT TO FLY ME BACK TO NEW YORK FAST.

IS IT THE CORE, SIR?

MAYBE. MAYBE SOME- THIN' WORSE.

WE'VE RECEIVED WORD THAT COMMANDER QUARTERMAIN IS NOT EXPECTED TO LAST OUT THE NIGHT.

MAKE THE NECESSARY ARRANGEMENTS.

THEY'VE ALREADY BEEN INITIATED.

VERY GOOD.

INTERESTING THAT NICHOLAS SHOULD LEAVE SO QUICKLY. IT IS A PITY WE'VE NEVER BEEN ABLE TO BREAK THAT *CODE* OF HIS.

WE'VE CERTAINLY TRIED. WHERE DO YOU THINK HE WAS HEADED?

I DON'T KNOW. BUT WE'LL KNOW SOON ENOUGH. WE ALWAYS DO.

New Jersey.

The Roxxon Industrial Research Complex.

A lone figure glides across the face of the moon...

...AND SILENTLY COMES TO A LANDING WITHIN THE COMPLEX.

BETTER DUCK BEHIND HERE. SEARCHLIGHT'S COMIN'.

THIS IS THE RENDEZVOUS POINT AND HE AIN'T HERE. *BLAST!* HE SAID HE'D BE HERE AT 0200 HOURS. I TRAINED HIM -- I TRAINED ALL OF 'EM -- THEY KNOW YOU CAN'T GET SLOPPY IN THIS BUSINESS!

CALM DOWN, FURY. WHAT ARE YOU DOIN', GETTIN' *CROTCHETY* IN YOUR OLD AGE? FACE IT, YOUR NERVES HAVE BEEN TOO FRAZZLED FOR ONE DAY.

EH?

IF YOU'RE GONNA BE SNEAKIN' UP ON NICK FURY, YOU'RE GONNA HAVE TO DO BETTER THAN THAT, *ROLLINS!*

OOOOOFF

THUMPFF

I'M SORRY. I MUST BE A BIT RUSTY.

THAT'S NO EXCUSE, ROLLINS. YOU SENT ME A CODE 1A ALARM, SON, INDICATIN' THAT *SHIELD* HAS BEEN *INFILTRATED* BY ENEMY AGENTS. THAT'S A MIGHTY SERIOUS CHARGE TO MAKE...

...BUT AFTER WHAT HAPPENED TODAY, I CAN ACCEPT *ANYTHING*. YOU KNOW ABOUT THE CORE?

HERE, PUT ON THIS WORKER'S UNIFORM. *HURRY*, SIR, WE DON'T HAVE MUCH TIME.

AND...

OKAY, ROLLINS, YOU'RE ONE OF MY BEST SLEEPER AGENTS. IF YOU TELL ME I SHOULD BE WORRIED, I'M *WORRIED*. SO TELL ME, WHAT'S BEEN GOIN' ON?

AS YOU KNOW, ROXXON'S BEEN ENGAGED IN SEVERAL ILLEGAL AND DANGEROUS ACTIVITIES IN THE PAST FEW YEARS.

YOU DIDN'T WANT THAT TO HAPPEN AGAIN WITHOUT *SHIELD* BEING AWARE OF IT, SO USING MY AREA OF EXPERTISE-- *COMPUTERS*--AS COVER, I GOT A JOB HERE AS A *PROGRAMMER*.

NEXT YOU'RE GONNA TELL ME YOU'RE ONE OF MY HANDPICKED PERSONAL SPIES WHO ANSWERS ONLY TO ME AND NO ONE ELSE. LET'S GET TO IT, ROLLINS, TELL ME SOMETHIN' I *DON'T* KNOW.

YESSIR, I ROSE QUICKLY THROUGH THE RANKS, BEING SOMETHING OF A COMPUTER WHIZ KID, BUT I DETECTED NO SIGNS OF ANY *ILLEGAL ACTIVITIES*. THEN, A FEW MONTHS AGO, I BEGAN HEARING ABOUT A TOP SECRET PROGRAM, CODE NAMED *DELTA*. ENORMOUS EXPENDITURES WERE BEING CHANNELED INTO IT, BUT I COULDN'T DISCOVER WHAT DELTA WAS OR WHAT IT DID.

DELTA? FUNNY... *SHIELD* HAD A PROGRAM PROPOSAL LABELED THAT... SOMETHIN' ABOUT *AGENT RE-TRAININ'*... NEVER GOT OFF THE GROUND. SO MUCH FOR *ORIGINALITY*.

YESSIR! A FEW MONTHS AGO, I FINALLY SUCCEEEDED IN BEING ASSIGNED TO A LOW LEVEL DELTA SECURITY AREA. IT SEEMED TO BE JUST ANOTHER ENERGY RESEARCH PROGRAM, BUT I DISCOVERED THAT ALMOST ALL OF THE DELTA COMPUTER PROGRAM WAS BLOCKED OFF FROM ITS PROGRAMMERS.

IT TOOK ME SEVERAL MONTHS, BUT I WAS FINALLY ABLE TO BREAK THE *CODE*...

VERY GOOD, ROLLINS. SOMETHING *NEW* ABOUT TIME.

WHAT DID YOU FIND WHEN YOU ENTERED THE DELTA PROGRAM?

COLONEL, IT'S--

FREEZE!

JUST WHAT WE NEED

ALL RIGHT, YOU TWO, THIS IS A RESTRICTED AREA. SHOW ME YOUR I.D.

HEY, NO PROBLEM.

I THINK YOU'LL FIND EVERYTHING IN ORDER.

YEAH-- SORRY. BUT YOU GUYS KNOW NOBODY'S SUPPOSED TO BE IN THIS QUADRANT, ESPECIALLY SINCE YOU'RE FROM DELTA.

...YOU'LL HAVE TO COME WITH ME!

SORRY, FRIEND, NO CAN DO!

THWOK

ODD. THERE WAS NO SCHEDULED SECURITY SWEEP FOR TONIGHT.

WELL, WE CAN'T LET THIS JOKER REPORT THAT HE SAW US--IT WOULD KINDA BLOW OUR LITTLE COVERT OPERATION HERE.

EVER HEAR OF A POP QUIZ, JACK?

SO WE GOTTA MAKE HIM FORGET HE SAW ANYTHING.

THE GAFF'S BOYS JUST CAME UP WITH THIS MINI-BRAIN SCANNER, WIPES A PERSON'S MEMORY OF THE PAST TWO HOURS RIGHT OUTTA HIS HEAD.

INCREDIBLE!

YEAH, AIN'T IT? THE COUNCIL ORDERED IT ISSUED TO ALL HIGH LEVEL OPERATIVES. IT'S STILL EXPERIMENTAL-- BUT NOW WE CAN TAKE YER THOUGHTS FROM YA!

IMPRESSIVE, HUH?

IS THERE ANY PERMANENT DAMAGE, COLONEL?

I WAS TOLD IT WASN'T POLITE TA ASK.

Shortly...

SO, THIS IS *DELTA*, HUH? MIND TELLIN' ME WHERE EVERYBODY IS?

DELTA PERSONNEL ARE KEPT TO A MINIMUM, COLONEL, FOR SECURITY REASONS. BUT ALL LOW SECURITY CLEARANCE PERSONNEL WERE ORDERED *NOT* TO REPORT IN TONIGHT. I DON'T KNOW WHY. WE'RE NOT EXPECTED TO ASK QUESTIONS.

THEN AIN'T IT *RISKY* BEIN' HERE TONIGHT?

NOT REALLY, SIR. ONCE I PUNCH IN THE RIGHT ACCESS CODE, THE DELTA COMPUTER WILL REGISTER US AS A PRE-ARRANGED SECURITY PATROL. I PROGRAMMED THE AUTHORIZATION INTO THE COMPUTER MYSELF.

GOOD GOIN', ROLLINS.

THANK YOU, SIR. BUT I'M ONLY DOIN' WHAT YOU TRAINED ME TO DO: BY BECOMING TOTALLY FAMILIAR WITH MY ASSIGNED ENVIRONMENT, I CAN EFFECTIVELY ASSIMILATE ALL INFORM--

ER... ROLLINS, COULD YOU PUT A *LID* ON IT? WHAT'S WITH YOU KIDS TODAY ANYWAY? DO YOU ACTUALLY *LIKE* RECITIN' RULES AND REGULATIONS?

PROJECT DELTA

I NEVER REALLY GAVE IT MUCH THOUGHT, SIR. NOW STAND BACK WHILE THE SCANNERS CONFIRM MY HANDPRINTS AND VOILA--

-- WELCOME TO MY HUMBLE *OFFICE*, SIR.

VERY IMPRESSIVE, JACK. I DOUBT *SHIELD* COULD DO BETTER.

INTERESTING YOU SHOULD SAY THAT, COLONEL. FOLLOW ME.

THIS LOOKS LIKE A *SURVEILLANCE* OPERATION TA ME. HAS ROXXON BEEN EAVESDROPPIN' ON SATELLITE SIGNALS? THESE BOYS HAVE DONE WORSE.

OH, IT'S WORSE THAN THAT, SIR.

I'M ORDERING THE COMPUTER TO DISPLAY AND REPORT ON ITS PRIMARY FILE. WATCH THE *SCREEN.*

WHAT TH--? THAT'S THE *SHIELD* INSIGNIA!

SUPREME HEADQUARTERS INTERNATIONAL ESPIONAGE LAW-ENFORCEMENT DIVISION IS AN EXTRA-GOVERNMENTAL INTERNATIONAL INTELLIGENCE AND SECURITY AGENCY...

...THERE ARE 4,232 *SHIELD* OPERATIVES IN THE U.S.A. ALONE. PERSONNEL FILES DISPLAYED HERE REVEAL--

L JONES

GAIL RU

DE FONTAINE

SYDNEYE. LE THE GAB

JAMES

ROLLINS, HOW IN *BLAZES* DID THEY GET THIS INFORMATION? THESE PEOPLE ARE CLASSIFIED!

-- THE HELICARRIER WAS ARMORED WITH A TRIPLE HULL OF FIVE INCH HARDENED ALLOY, THEN A TWELVE INCH LAYER OF HIGH SPEED--

HELICARRIER

NOBODY BUT *SHIELD* IS SUPPOSED TA HAVE THIS STUFF!

VIEW AFT

I KNOW.

THE POWER CORE IS A HIGHLY UNSTABLE ENERGY SOURCE, DEVELOPED IN 1961 BY A--

POWER CORE

THE CORE! THEY'VE GOT THE FILE ON THE *CORE!* BUT THAT AIN'T POSSIBLE-- NOBODY BUT *ME* HAS ACCESS TO THAT FILE!

WHAT'S THAT?

SOMETHING'S GOING ON DEEP DOWN IN DELTA, COLONEL--

THEN LET'S GO. I WANNA SEE WHAT'S *GOIN' ON* IN THIS PLACE.

I'VE ONLY BEEN DOWN THERE ONCE. IT'LL BE DANGEROUS GOING THAT FAR...

BRRRAANGG

I AIN'T INTERESTED IN EXCUSES, ROLLINS, I WANT ANSWERS!

THE PRIZE HAS BEEN SECURED.

EXCELLENT.

THERE IS A REPORT OF A BRIEF POWER SURGE IN THE COMPLEX SOME MOMENTS BEFORE THE CORE'S ARRIVAL. IT IS LISTED AS A ROUTINE SECURITY CHECK.

INVESTIGATE IT ANYWAY. WE CAN ALLOW NOTHING TO GO WRONG NOW.

"BY THE WAY, HAS THERE BEEN ANY NEWS ON NICHOLAS' WHEREABOUTS?

"NO, AND I FIND THAT DISCONCERTING. MIGHT I SUGGEST CLOSER SURVEILLANCE?

"PERHAPS.

"BUT NICHOLAS HAS ALWAYS BEEN A FREE SPIRIT--

"--OR--

"--SO HE'S BEEN LED TO BELIEVE."

NICHOLAS HAS TRANSMITTED A SUMMONING BEAM. HE WISHES TO CONVERSE WITH THE BOARD, PRIORITY ONE-A.

INTERESTING.

NEW YORK CITY. DAWN.

IT WILL BE SEVERAL HOURS BEFORE MOST OF THESE BUILDINGS COME ALIVE WITH THE GREAT INFLUX OF OFFICE WORKERS...

...BUT ONE BUILDING NEVER SLEEPS. ONE BUILDING NEVER STANDS EMPTY. FOR TWENTY FOUR HOURS A DAY, SEVEN DAYS A WEEK, THIS BUILDING HUMS WITH ACTIVITY...

...FOR THIS BUILDING HOUSES THE WORLD HEADQUARTERS OF THE SUPREME HEADQUARTERS INTERNATIONAL ESPIONAGE LAW-ENFORCEMENT DIVISION.

SHIELD

FOR THIS BUILDING IS SHIELD CENTRAL!

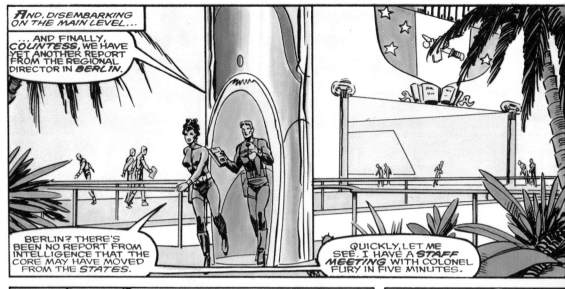

AND, DISEMBARKING ON THE MAIN LEVEL...

...AND FINALLY, *COUNTESS*, WE HAVE YET ANOTHER REPORT FROM THE REGIONAL DIRECTOR IN *BERLIN*.

BERLIN? THERE'S BEEN NO REPORT FROM INTELLIGENCE THAT THE CORE MAY HAVE MOVED FROM THE *STATES*.

QUICKLY, LET ME SEE. I HAVE A *STAFF MEETING* WITH COLONEL FURY IN FIVE MINUTES.

WHY HE'S MERELY DISPATCHING STANDARD RECON TEAMS THROUGHOUT GERMANY. ODD HE'D FILE SUCH A *MUNDANE REPORT*.

THEY'VE BEEN EXTREMELY *EFFICIENT* IN BERLIN LATELY.

WELL, THE *WILHELM* I KNOW HATES TO FILE DISPATCHES. HAVE YOU SEEN...

COMMANDER DUGAN? NEVER MIND.

WOULD YOU *FURSHSLUGGIN'* KIDS *BACK OFF* AND GIVE A MAN ROOM TO THINK?!

NOW, NOW, DUM DUM.

OH, HI, *VAL*. THESE KIDS! FRESH OUTTA COLLEGE, ALL THEY WANNA DO IS REPORT, FILE, AND REPORT ON THE *FILIN'!*

DON'T ANYONE WANNA GO OUT AND FIGHT *BAD GUYS* NO MORE?

I SWEAR WE GOT US A BUILDING FULL OF *ACCOUNTANTS*--

WHY'S IT SO *DARK* IN HERE?

JASPER?

VAL, DUM DUM...I...I JUST GOT *WORD*... CLAY DIED LAST NIGHT...

"...HOW ARE WE GOING TO TELL THE *DIRECTOR?*"

CRAZY FOOL! DOES HE WANT TO KILL HIMSELF? DRIVING THAT *FAST*--

SCREECHH

"--INTO AN ALLEY!"

VVIIPP

HOLOGRAM STILL GIVES ME THE *CHILLS!* ONE OF THESE DAYS I *KNOW* I'M GONNA SLAM INTO A *REAL* BRICK WALL!

U556

PREPARE FOR VOICE AND RETINA IDENTIFICATION.

IDENTIFY.

FURY, NICHOLAS. CODE NUMBER L-1.

INCOMPLETE RETINA SCAN: DISPLAY LEFT·EYE:

BLASTED CONTRAPTION! I ONLY *GOT* ONE EYE!

SCAN MEDICAL FILES: CONFIRMED. PROCEED RETINA VOICE PRINT CONFIRMED.

RETINA SCAN (RIGHT EYE ONLY) CONFIRMED. IDENTIFY CONFIRMED.

GOOD MORNING, DIRECTOR FURY. HAVE A NICE DAY.

GEE, *THANKS.*

COLONEL

MIDDLE EAST REVENUE FIGURES

SOVIET ACTIVITIES

INTELLIGENCE SAYS

POWER CORE

IN A DARKENED MEETING ROOM...

I–I JUST CAN'T BELIEVE IT, *DUM DUM*. I KNOW WE'RE TRAINED TO EXPECT THESE THINGS, BUT...

I KNOW, *COUNTESS*, BELIEVE ME, NO ONE IS TAKIN' THIS WELL. HOW ARE THE ARRANGEMENTS COMIN', *JASPER*?

AS WELL AS CAN BE EXPECTED. I NEVER LIKED HANDLING THESE AFFAIRS, YOU KNOW. IT'S VERY UNPLEASANT.

NICK! YOU'RE HERE!

WHA--? *VAL?* YOU LOOK LIKE YOU'VE BEEN CR--

NICK... IT'S *CLAY*... WE RECEIVED WORD LAST NIGHT THAT... OH, NICK, I'M SO SORRY--BUT... CLAY *DIED* LAST NIGHT.

NICK?

NICK, ARE YOU ALL RIGHT?

NICK, 'OL BUDDY, DIDN'T YOU *HEAR* VAL? IT'S CLAY. HE DIDN'T MAKE IT.

ER--UM-- SIR, PERHAPS YOU'D LIKE A STATUS REPORT ON THE SEARCH FOR THE CORE?

INTERESTINGLY, ER... NEITHER *HYDRA* NOR *AIM* HAVE MADE ANY MOVES NOW THAT THEY POSSESS THE CORE. ALL DIVISIONS ARE ON FULL ALERT, WITH A WORLD-WIDE INTENSIVE SEARCH UNDERWAY...

SITWELL, SCHEDULE A FULL *STAFF MEETING* FOR 1200 HOURS..I WANT ALL THE INFO YOU HAVE ON *AIM*, *HYDRA* AND *ROXXON*.

AND WHEN I SAY ALL, I MEAN *ALL!*

NICK, WAIT!

HE DIDN'T EVEN RESPOND TO CLAY'S DEATH... IT WAS AS IF HE WERE A HUNDRED MILES AWAY.

I MUST AGREE, I'VE NEVER SEEN THE COLONEL SO *IMPASSIVE*.

IMPASSIVE, JUNIOR? YOU GOT IT ALL WRONG. WHAT WE SAW WAS A MAN *ON THE EDGE*... AN' I AIN'T *NEVER* SEEN NICK FURY THAT WAY BEFORE!

AND OUTSIDE, IN THE CORRIDOR...

GOOD MORNING, SIR. I HAVE THAT REPORT YOU...

HE COMPLETELY *IGNORED* ME! I GUESS MR. HIGH AND MIGHTY CAN'T BE BOTHERED.

BUT IT IS A DIFFERENT NICK FURY WHO ENTERS A SIDE CORRIDOR A FEW MOMENTS LATER...

I DON'T BELIEVE IT. I DON'T *WANNA* BELIEVE IT.

CLAY'S DEAD.

I'VE BEEN SO WORKED UP ABOUT ROXXON AND DELTA FOR THE PAST FEW HOURS, I ALMOST *FORGOT* ABOUT CLAY! WHAT KIND OF MAN ARE *YOU*, FURY? IS *SHIELD* THE ONLY THING THAT MATTERS TO YOU ANY MORE?

IT'S ALMOST TIME FOR THE BOARD TO CALL...

SO THROW AWAY YOUR CRYIN' TOWEL, FURY, AND START ACTIN' LIKE A *SOLDIER*...

YESTERDAY, I WUZ THINKIN' ABOUT *RETIRIN'*, MEBBE TAKIN' VAL OFF SOMEWHERE TO LIVE SOMEWHERE LIKE *NORMAL PEOPLE* FOR A CHANGE. CLAY THOUGHT I WAS NUTS..., AND NOW HE'S DEAD...

YA CAN WORRY TOMORROW. THERE'S *ALWAYS* A TOMORROW.

SURE. JUST ASK CLAY QUARTERMAIN.

EXERCISE ROOM

AND AS NICK WALKS OFF, HE PASSES ONE OF THE SHIELD COMPLEX'S MANY TRAINING CHAMBERS...

...WHERE TWO OF HIS CLOSEST ASSOCIATES, *JIMMY WOO* AND *GABE JONES*, ARE ENGAGED IN A LITTLE EARLY MORNING WORK-OUT...

HAAIEEE!

OOOF!

YOU'RE NOT PRESENTING MUCH OF A *CHALLENGE*, THIS MORNING, GABE.

SORRY, JIMMY. MY HEART'S NOT IN IT TODAY. I CAN'T STOP THINKING ABOUT *CLAY.*

WE WORK IN A DANGEROUS BUSINESS, GABE. CASUALTIES ARE TO BE EXPECTED, HOWEVER UNFORTUNATE.

AREN'T YOU BEING A LITTLE *COLD,* BUDDY? CLAY WAS OUR FRIEND.

MAYBE YOU *HAVE* TO BE COLD IN ORDER TO BE AN AGENT OF *SHIELD.* MAYBE IT'S THE ONLY WAY YOU CAN SURVIVE.

ENTERING A HIGH-SPEED PERSONNEL CARRIER, THE TWO AGENTS ARE CARRIED MANY LEVELS ABOVE TO THE COMPLEX'S LIVING QUARTERS...

...WHERE THEY ARE GREETED BY...

NICK!

WHAT ARE YOU TWO LOLLYGAGGIN' AROUND FOR? AND GET IN UNIFORM... YOU *KNOW* THE REGULATIONS!

NICK, WE DON'T GO ON DUTY TILL--

I DON'T THINK HE WAS INTERESTED IN ANY EXCUSES.

I'VE KNOWN NICK SINCE WE SERVED IN THE *HOWLERS* TOGETHER, JIMMY. HE'S *NEVER* TAKEN THE LOSS OF A MAN WELL.

SHORTLY, IN FURY'S PRIVATE OFFICE...

GOD HELP ME...

...CLAY'S DEAD.

WHAT'S GOIN' ON? NONE OF IT SEEMS REAL... CLAY DEAD... THE POWER CORE... SHIELD SECRETS RIPPED OFF LIKE THEY WERE PUBLISHED IN YESTERDAY'S PAPER...

NICK, HOW DID YOU LET THINGS GET SO MESSED UP? HOW? WHO KNOWS? ALL I KNOW IS THAT I'M TOO TIRED... TOO OLD... TA GO ON FIGHTIN' THE WORLD'S BATTLES EVERY DAY. I'M SICK OF IT. I'M SICK OF SEEING MY FRIENDS DIE. I'M SICK OF IT ALL.

THERE GO THE LIGHTS. THEY'RE ON TIME... THEY'RE ALWAYS ON TIME.

GOOD AFTERNOON, NICHOLAS. WE MUST ADMIT SOME SURPRISE AT YOUR REQUEST FOR THIS MEETING. YOU SELDOM CALL FOR A BOARD MEETING.

YEAH, WELL, I NEVER DID LIKE TALKIN' TA MEN I AIN'T EVEN ALLOWED TO SEE.

COME NOW, NICK, YOU REALIZE THE NEED FOR SECRECY.

LISTEN, I'LL GET RIGHT TO THE POINT. THE POWER CORE AIN'T WITH *HYDRA* OR *AIM* LIKE WE THOUGHT. IT'S AT A ROXXON RESEARCH PLANT IN JERSEY. ROXXON HAS A SURVEILLANCE PROJECT CALLED *DELTA* THAT'S BROKEN INTO OUR *COMPUTER RECORDS*...

WE CAN'T ALLOW A SECURITY BREACH LIKE THIS TO CONTINUE. THEY MAY BE SHARIN' OUR RECORDS WITH *AIM* OR *HYDRA*. OUR ENTIRE *OPERATION* IS IN JEOPARDY.

I LOST GOOD MEN IN THE CORE RAID. GOOD AGENTS. I WANT AUTHORIZATION FOR A FULL-SCALE NON-MILITARY TAKEOVER OF ROXXON...

... I WANT TO SEE THOSE *MURDERERS PAY!*

NICHOLAS, YOUR FINDINGS ARE EXTREMELY *ALARMING.* IF ROXXON THREATENS *SHIELD* SECURITY, THEN IT MUST BE *DEALT* WITH. WE WILL CONFER AND FORMULATE A PLAN. IN THE MEANTIME, TELL *NO ON* OF THESE DEVELOPMENTS.

WAITAMINIT... I'M TALKIN' *MAJOR DISASTER* HERE... OUR SECURITY SYSTEMS HAVE BEEN RAIDED... WE CAN'T AFFORD TO *WASTE TIME--*

GOOD AFTERNOON, NICK.

GOOD-- AFTERNOON?

CRASH

WHAT ARE YOU *TALKIN'* ABOUT? EVERYTHIN' MIGHT COME CRASHIN' AROUND OUR EARS AN' YOU ACT LIKE I'VE GONE *OVER BUDGET!* WHAT'S GOIN' ON?

AND WHAT'S WORSE IS THAT YOU'RE GONNA WAIT FOR THEIR ORDERS BECAUSE THAT'S WHAT YOU'VE *SWORN* TA DO... LISTEN TO A BUNCHA SHADOWS... ACT LIKE A *GOOD SOLDIER*...

GOD HELP ME.

CLAY IS DEAD.

AND IN THE HIDDEN BOARD ROOM...

THIS IS TRULY SERIOUS. HOW COULD NICHOLAS HAVE DISCOVERED SO *MUCH* IN SO SHORT A PERIOD OF TIME?

WE UNDERESTIMATED HIM. WE HAVE NEVER DOUBTED HIS *BRILLIANCE--* THAT IS ONE OF THE REASONS WE APPOINTED HIM AS DIRECTOR OF *SHIELD. WE* MAY HAVE GOTTEN SLOPPY IN RECENT YEARS.

IT IS FORTUNATE THAT NICHOLAS HAS NO IDEA WHAT DELTA *TRULY* IS. THAT IS OUR ADVANTAGE. BUT HE IS NO *FOOL.* HE WILL BEGIN A FULL-SCALE PROBE. I DO NOT KNOW IF EVEN OUR *WALL OF DECEPTION* COULD SURVIVE SUCH AN INVESTIGATION.

NEEDLESS TO SAY, IT IS A RISK *I* REFUSE TO TAKE.

IT'S OBVIOUS HE HAS ONE OF HIS SLEEPER AGENTS STATIONED AT ROXXON. WE SHOULD NEVER HAVE ALLOWED HIM THE LUXURY OF TRAINING A CADRE OF *AGENTS* ANSWERABLE ONLY TO HIM.

HINDSIGHT IS A WONDERFUL THING. MAKE SURE THIS SLEEPER AGENT DISCOVERS *NOTHING ELSE.*

CONSIDER IT DONE.

ROXXON. A SHORT TIME LATER...

OF ALL THE *STUPID STUNTS*, THIS BEATS ALL.

COLONEL FURY SAID HE'D BE SENDING IN MORE UNDERCOVER AGENTS TO *HELP* ME, BUT I NEVER EXPECTED THIS! DOES HE WANT TO BLOW *EVERYTHING?*

HOW COULD *SHIELD* CONTACT ME ON MY COMMUNICATOR *HERE?* TRANSMISSION LIKE THAT CAN BE EASILY *TRACED!* IT'S SHEER INCOMPETENCE!

THIS IS WHERE I'M SUPPOSED TO MEET MY CONTACT. MAYBE HE CAN EXPLAIN WHAT'S GOING ON!

STORE ROOM

ANYBODY HERE? I-- WHA--?

NO!

FZZATT

I'M SORRY, ROLLINS. YOU MUST BELIEVE THAT.

BUT WE MUST ALL PERFORM DISTATEFUL DEEDS WHEN THE SECURITY OF *SHIELD* IS AT STAKE.

...AS WE KNOW, THE POSSIBILITY OF A REUNIFICATION BETWEEN *AIM* AND *HYDRA* HAS ALWAYS BEEN A THEORETICAL POSSIBILITY.

DESPITE THE POLITICAL DIFFERENCES THAT EXIST BETWEEN THEM. THIS POSSIBILITY HAS BECOME ALL THE MORE TANGIBLE SINCE THE DEATH OF *MODOK, AIM'S* RENEGADE LEADER.

IF, AS ALL EVIDENCE SUGGESTS, THESE TWO SUPER-ORGANIZATIONS HAVE JOINED FORCES TO HARNESS THE ENERGY OF THE *POWER CORE...*

...THEN *SHIELD* CLEARLY FACES ITS MOST DANGEROUS THREAT SINCE *HYDRA* WAS FOUNDED BY THE NAZI MADMAN, *BARON WOLFGANG von STRUCKER.*

GOOD WORK, JASPER. NOW GIVE US EVERYTHING YOU KNOW ON *ROXXON.*

ATTENTION, COLONEL FURY. BY ORDER OF THE BOARD, YOUR PRESENCE IS REQUIRED IN THE *INTERROGATION* CHAMBER. PRIORITY 1A. REPORT *UNARMED.*

WHA--?

NICK, WHAT'S WRONG? WHY DO THEY WANT YOU IN THE INTERROGATION CHAMBER?

DON'T LOOK SO WORRIED, YOU OL' WALRUS. YOU KNOW HOW THOSE MYSTERY MEN LOVE *THEATRICS.* I'LL BE BACK.

I DON'T LIKE THIS. THE BOARD'S NEVER BEEN THIS DIRECT BEFORE-- INTERRUPTIN' A GENERAL STAFF MEETING. AND *WHY* DO THEY WANT ME *UNARMED?*

NOPE, I DON'T LIKE THIS AT ALL.

ARE THEY TRYIN' TO MAKE ME FEEL LIKE A *BAD SCHOOL BOY* OR SOMETHIN'? WOULDN'T SURPRISE ME... THEY'RE ALWAYS WILLIN' TO SHOW WHO'S BOSS.

INTERROGATION CHAMBER, LEVEL 22.

WITHIN SECONDS, THE CARRIER ARRIVES AT THE CHAMBER...

WELL, HERE I AM. LOOKS LIKE THEY'VE SET UP THE *WORKS* ALL RIGHT.

FUNNY, I NEVER THOUGHT I'D BE ON *THIS* SIDE OF THE DAIS.

CAN'T SAY I LIKE THE FEELING.

HERE THEY ARE, LIKE CLOCKWORK.

COLONEL FURY, WE HAVE *INVESTIGATED* YOUR ALLEGATIONS REGARDING THE ROXXON CORPORATION. WE FIND *NO EVIDENCE* TO SUBSTANTIATE ANY OF YOUR CLAIMS.

WHAT? THAT'S CRAZY! I SAW THE EVIDENCE WITH *MY OWN EYES!* I SAW THE CORE! MY AGENT SPENT *MONTHS* BREAKIN' INTO DELTA!

AH, YES. YOUR COVER AGENT. *AGENT ROLLINS,* WAS IT NOT?

WAITAMINNIT! I NEVER TOLD YOU HIS NAME. NOBODY BUT *ME* KNEW HE WAS THERE. HOW DID...

COLONEL, YOU SHOULD KNOW BY NOW...

...THAT THE BOARD IS AWARE OF *EVERYTHING* WE DO.

ROLLINS!

A DIRECT ORDER, THEY SAY. YEAH, JUST LIKE ALL THOSE DIRECT ORDERS I DISOBEYED FROM HAPPY SAM.

CAPT SAM SA

WHEN DID YOU *START* BEIN' THE GOOD SOLDIER, NICK? WHEN DID YOU *STOP* QUESTIONIN' THINGS? WHEN DID YOU GET OLD?

AND CLAY IS DEAD. AND SOMEHOW, SOMEWAY THOSE *BUZZAROS* UP THERE ARE INVOLVED.

COLONEL, WE HAVE OUR ORDERS.

Y'KNOW, JACKIE, I'VE TRAINED MY AGENTS TO BE GOOD SOLDIERS, TO FOLLOW ORDERS, BECAUSE I NEVER DOUBTED THAT WE WERE ON THE *RIGHT SIDE*. I AIN'T SO SURE ABOUT THAT ANYMORE...

...SO I SAY *NUTS* TO BEIN' THE GOOD SOLDIER.

ARRGH! KAPOW

NICHOLAS, DON'T BE *FOOLISH*. YOU CANNOT ESCAPE. WE WILL SOUND THE GENERAL ALARM.

AWW, STICK IT IN YER *EAR!*

ALERT! ALERT! BY ORDERS OF THE BOARD, COLONEL NICHOLAS FURY IS TO BE APPREHENDED FOR QUESTIONING!

I DON'T UNDERSTAND! HAS THE WHOLE WORLD GONE *INSANE*? WHAT HAS NICK DONE?

I DON'T KNOW, COUNTESS, BUT--

GABE'S RIGHT, JASPER. NICK FURY WOULD NO SOONER BETRAY *SHIELD* THAN I WOULD KISS MY MOTHER-IN-LAW.

HOLD ON THERE, JASPER. THERE'S NO NEED TO GO FOR YOUR *GUN!* THIS IS PROBABLY SOME RIDICULOUS *MISTAKE!*

NICK FURY *TRAINED* ME, BLAST IT! HE TOLD ME WHAT DUTY AND LOYALTY TO *SHIELD* MEANT, AND IF *SHIELD* ORDERS ME TO ARREST MY COMMANDING OFFICER...

...THEN I WILL DO SO BECAUSE NICK FURY WOULD WANT IT *NO OTHER WAY!*

DUM DUM, THERE'S NO WAY OF FINDING OUT WHAT HAS HAPPENED UNTIL WE *TALK* TO NICK...

...AND IF ANYONE HAS TO ARREST HIM I'D RATHER IT BE *US* INSTEADA SOME TRIGGER-HAPPY ROOKIE.

AMEN.

ALERT! ALERT. ALL AGENTS RED ALERT!

THEN LET'S GO!

HEY, JASPER-- WAIT UP FER US!

AND SEVERAL LEVELS BELOW, IN A DARKENED CORRIDOR...

AN ESCAPE LIFT... A HIGH SPEED ELEVATOR THAT COULD GET ME TO STREET LEVEL IN SECONDS. IF I CAN *REACH* IT, I CAN GET OUT OF THIS PLACE AND CONTACT THE *AVENGERS* OR SOMEBODY. I'M DEFINITELY GONNA NEED *HELP* ON THIS ONE.

ALL CLEAR.

C'MON, FURY! EVERY SECOND COUNTS!

GOTTA ACTIVATE THE HATCH.

SMASH

EMERGENCY ELEVATOR

NOBODY'S AROUND.

WHHHIRRR

NOW A QUICK LEAP AND-- *UH-OH*.

COLONEL, I SUGGEST YOU STOP RIGHT THERE!

EMERGENCY ELEVATOR

I HAVE MY ORDERS TO BRING YOU IN.

I AM A LOYAL AGENT OF *SHIELD*, COLONEL, AND I ASSURE YOU I WILL NOT ALLOW YOU TO *ESCAPE*.

ROLLINS! WHAT *HAPPENED* TO YOU, JACKIE? WERE YOU ALWAYS WORKIN' FOR THE BOARD COVERIN' UP THEIR *DIRTY TRICKS?*

ROLLINS! WHAT'S GOIN' ON HERE!?!

DUM DUM!

COLONEL FURY IS BEING ARRESTED FOR *TREASON*, COMMANDER DUGAN--

--BY ORDER OF THE BOARD.

ROLLINS IS SQUEEZIN' THE TRIGGER! DUM DUM, I HOPE YOUR EYESIGHT AIN'T GOIN'!

ROLLINS! NO!

SPIRAK

FZZATT

YOU IDIOT!

I AIN'T LETTIN' YOU SHOOT AN *UNARMED MAN!*

ROLLIN'S SHOT HIT A *POWER LINE*...SCATTERED EVERYONE. BUT HE'S NOT OUT. I GOTTA BE *QUICK.*

COLONEL, YOU WON'T LUCK OUT A *SECOND* TIME. YOU ARE A DANGER TO *SHIELD.*

ROLLINS, WHAT ARE YOU *TALKIN'* ABOUT?

I'M A SITTIN' DUCK UP HERE. WHERE IS THAT-- AH, THERE YOU ARE.

THIS MAGNESIUM PELLET STOPPED A *HYDRA* AGENT THE OTHER DAY. I FIGGER WHAT WORKS ON ONE SLUG SHOULD WORK ON ANOTHER.

FWWISSS

ARRGHH!

NO TIME TO WASTE. GOTTA ACTIVATE THIS BLASTED *CONTRAPTION--*

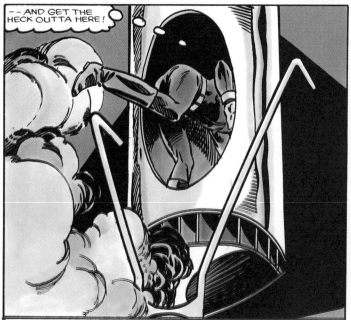

--AND GET THE HECK OUTTA HERE!

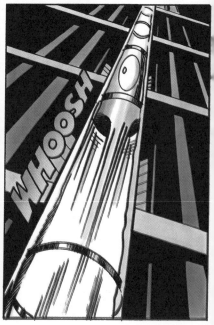

WHOOSH

YOU *OLD FOOL!* WHO ARE YOU TO DISOBEY A DIRECT ORDER FROM THE BOARD? *GUARDS,* PLACE COMMANDER DUGAN UNDER ARREST!

NOW HOLD ON HERE!

IT'S ALL RIGHT, GABE. I CAN HANDLE THIS.

ALL OF FURY'S CLOSE ASSOCIATES WILL BE PUT UNDER SURVEILLANCE, JONES. SO I SUGGEST *YOU* WATCH YOUR STEP, *OLD MAN.*

AND YOU WATCH WHO YOU *THREATEN,* SON.

DO YOU WANT TO JOIN YOUR FRIEND, JONES? EVERYONE IN *SHIELD* KNOWS HOW YOU OLD HOWLERS LIKE TO STICK TOGETHER.

AH, *WOO,* THERE YOU ARE. THE SITUATION IS NOT GOOD!

THINGS ARE ACTUALLY GOING BETTER THAN EXPECTED. TOUCH YOUR LIP.

BLOOD?

FROM FURY'S PUNCH. YOU SEE, THINGS GO WELL. AS FOR NICK FURY...

"...HOW FAR CAN HE GO WITH ALL OF *SHIELD* AFTER HIM?"

"NOT FAR, NOT FAR AT ALL."

"You don't understand, babe. They want me dead.
Listen to me, SHIELD is lies, Val . . . all lies."

chapter two: INTO THE DEPTHS

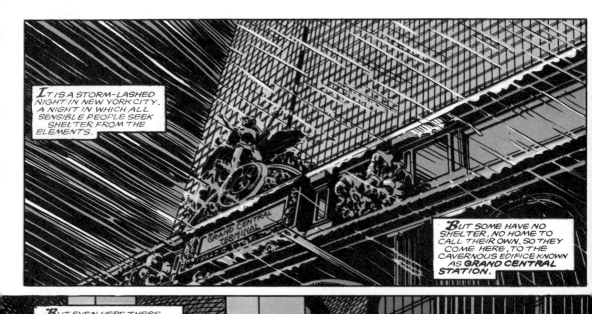

IT IS A STORM-LASHED NIGHT IN NEW YORK CITY. A NIGHT IN WHICH ALL SENSIBLE PEOPLE SEEK SHELTER FROM THE ELEMENTS.

BUT SOME HAVE NO SHELTER, NO HOME TO CALL THEIR OWN, SO THEY COME HERE, TO THE CAVERNOUS EDIFICE KNOWN AS GRAND CENTRAL STATION.

BUT EVEN HERE THESE UNFORTUNATES OFTEN FIND NO PEACE.

OKAY, FOLKS, UP AND AT 'EM, IT'S TIME TO MOVE ON. YOU KNOW YOU CAN'T STAY HERE.

JEEZ, SARGE, WHERE DO THEY ALL **COME** FROM?

ON NIGHTS LIKE THIS THEY CRAWL OUT OF THE WOODWORK, KID. BUT DON'T **WORRY** ABOUT 'EM, THEY'RE NOT WORTH IT.

AND, AS THE GROUP DISPERSES...

HEY, OLD MAN, YOU GOT A **LIGHT**? HA, HA, HA.

HE DIDN'T EVEN ANSWER YOU, LOUIE. I **HATE** UNFRIENDLY PEOPLE, 'SPECIALLY IF THEY'RE BUMS.

YEAH, I THINK SOMEONE OUGHTTA TEACH GRAMPS A **LESSON** IN MANNERS...

...AFTER ALL IT'S BEEN A **SLOOW** NIGHT. WHADDAYA SAY, BOYS?

ALL RIGHT!

55

GUY AIN'T TOO BRIGHT. AIN'T NO ONE TOLD HIM IT AIN'T **SAFE** TO GO DOWN ALL BY HIMSELF?

$70.0 OVERNIGH

MEN

AWW, THIS IS GONNA BE **TOO** EASY!

BELOW.

BENEATH GRAND
CENTRAL LIES
ANOTHER WORLD.
IT IS A WORLD OF
PIPES AND STEAM.
OF DIRT AND
FILTH. OF ENDLESS
TUNNELS AND
TWISTING MAZES.
IT IS A WORLD
WHERE RATS AND
VERMIN RUN
RAMPANT.

IT IS A WORLD WHERE
THE *FORGOTTEN* COME.
THEY HAVE GIVEN UP ON
LIFE ABOVE, AND HAVE
RETREATED *HERE* INTO
THE DARK, INTO THE
DEPTHS.

IT IS A PLACE NOT ONLY FOR
THOSE WHO HAVE NO HOMES...
BUT HAVE NO *HOPE* AS WELL.

AND EVERY SO OFTEN,
A *NEW* LOST SOUL
VENTURES DOWN HERE
AND FINDS HIMSELF
LOST IN THE DEPTHS...

HEY, *YOU!*
WHAT ARE YOU
DOIN' HERE? I
DON'T KNOW
YOU, DO I?

NO. I'M
NEW.
LET ME
ALONE.

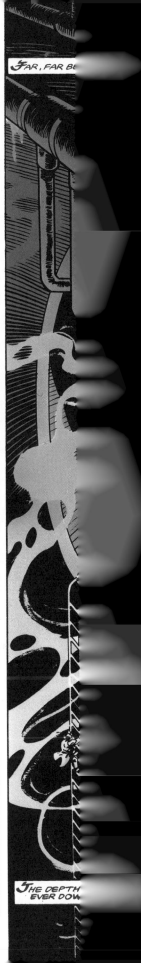

FAR, FAR BE

THE DEPTH
EVER DOW

HERE THE RATS AND VERMIN RULE. THIS IS THEIR PLACE.

NO ONE *EVER* COMES DOWN HERE. NOT EVEN THE LOST, THE HOPELESS, OR THE DESPERATE.

THAT IS... UNTIL TONIGHT.

A BRIGHT, GLOWING LIGHT SUDDENLY PUSHES BACK THE DARK. THE RATS RUN SCREECHING INTO THE SHADOWS. THEIR WORLD HAS BEEN INVADED.

PALMPRINT CONFIRMATION. ACCESS CODE EPSILON BETA SEVEN ENGAGED.

ENTRY PERMITTED.

THE DOOR CLOSES. THE LIGHT FADES.

AND THE DARK RETURNS.

INSIDE.

FLIP

CLIK

WELL, NICK, WHO'D A THOUGHT IT WOULD COME TO THIS?

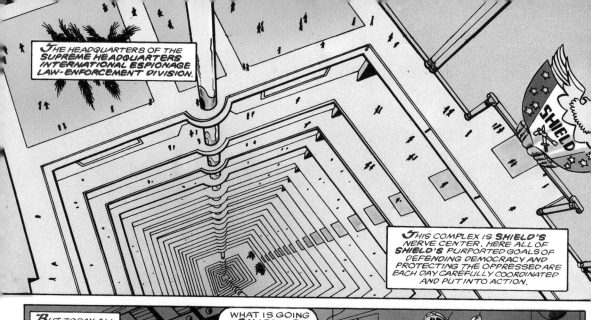

THE HEADQUARTERS OF THE *SUPREME HEADQUARTERS INTERNATIONAL ESPIONAGE LAW-ENFORCEMENT DIVISION.*

THIS COMPLEX IS *SHIELD'S* NERVE CENTER. HERE ALL OF *SHIELD'S* PURPORTED GOALS OF DEFENDING DEMOCRACY AND PROTECTING THE OPPRESSED ARE EACH DAY CAREFULLY COORDINATED AND PUT INTO ACTION.

BUT TODAY ALL IS NOT WELL.

THE DETENTION SECTION, CELL 1A, WHERE *THADDEUS "DUM DUM" DUGAN,* SHIELD'S SPECIAL DIRECTOR SITS IN CUSTODY...

WHAT IS GOING *ON* AROUND HERE?

HAS THE WHOLE WORLD GONE *CRAZY?* I DON'T UNDERSTAND WHAT'S HAPPENING. IT'S JUST PLAIN *RIDICULOUS!*

GABE, CALM DOWN! THIS AIN'T DOIN' YOUR BLOOD PRESSURE ANY GOOD.

YOU KNOW AS WELL AS *ME* WHY I'M HERE...

"YESTERDAY, WE WERE ORDERED TO *ARREST* NICK FURY, OUR OL' BUDDY AND *SHIELD'S* DIRECTOR, ON ORDERS OF THE COUNCIL, THE GUYS WHO *RUN* THIS SHOW. YOU AN' ME AN' THE COUNTESS *VALENTINA DE FONTAINE* COULDN'T BELIEVE OUR EARS... BUT WE DID WHAT WE *HAD* TO DO."

BUT WHEN *JACK ROLLINS,* ONE OF NICK'S PERSONAL AGENTS, WAS ABOUT TO *SHOOT* NICK, I JUMPED ROLLINS AND ALLOWED NICK TO ESCAPE. I DISOBEYED ORDERS, MR. JONES, AND *THAT'S* WHY I'M HERE!

ROLLINS! WHAT'S GOING **ON** WITH THAT GUY? WHY DID THE COUNCIL SUDDENLY GIVE HIM SO MUCH **AUTHORITY**? AND WHAT-- PLEASE TELL ME-- WAS NICK **CHARGED** WITH? WE **STILL** DON'T KNOW!

GABE, I AIN'T DENYIN' SOMETHIN' **BAD** AROUND HERE. BUT IT AIN'T THE **FIRST TIME** THAT WE HAVEN'T AGREED WITH **SHIELD** POLICY, AND IT PROBABLY WON'T BE THE **LAST!**

OH, YOU'LL BE AGREEING WITH OUR POLICIES VERY SOON, MR. DUGAN. **THAT** I CAN ASSURE YOU.

GOOD MORNING, GENTLEMEN.

ROLLINS!

WHAT DO YOU WANT, JACK?

I HAVE GOOD NEWS, DUM DUM. IN VIEW OF YOUR LONG SERVICE TO **SHIELD** AND THE ADMITTEDLY UNUSUAL EVENTS OF YESTERDAY, THE COUNCIL HAS DECIDED TO **DROP** ALL CHARGES AGAINST YOU.

STILL, BECAUSE THE CRISIS STILL THREATENS THE SECURITY OF **SHIELD**, YOU AND COMMANDER JONES ARE TO BE QUESTIONED BY THE COUNCIL.

NO ONE BUT **NICK** EVER SEES THE COUNCIL!

THE SITUATION HAS **CHANGED**, GABE. DON'T BE OBSTINATE. NOW, IF YOU'LL FOLLOW THE SECURITY TEAM, THE COUNCIL MEETING WILL BEGIN SHORTLY.

I'M **GOING**, ROLLINS. BUT I DON'T HAVE TO **LIKE** IT.

THEY WERE RIGHT. HE **IS** GOING TO BE A CHALLENGE.

SHIELD HQ...

DUM DUM! THANK GOODNESS THEY'VE RELEASED YOU!

THEY CAN'T KEEP AN OL' *HOWLER* LIKE ME DOWN, VAL. YOU SHOULD KNOW THAT FROM NICK. BUT LET'S GET CRACKIN' WHILE WE CAN... HAVE YOU HEARD ANYTHING?

APPARENTLY, WE'RE ALL UNDER *SUSPICION*, DUM DUM. IT'S A LOGICAL DEDUCTION ON THEIR PART, CONSIDERING OUR LONG SERVICE WITH COLONEL FURY. BUT WHAT IS IT WE'RE UNDER SUSPICION *FOR* IS BEYOND ME.

JASPER'S RIGHT. THEY'VE EVEN CALLED *ERIC KOENIG* IN FROM EUROPE. HE'S IN WITH THE COUNCIL NOW.

KOENIG, HUH? HE'S KNOWN NICK SINCE THE *WAR*. THEY'RE GATHERING THE PEOPLE NICK WAS *CLOSEST* TO. THEY MUST THINK HE *TOLD* US SOMETHIN'.

LOOK AT US. EVEN IN TIMES LIKE THESE, WE'RE MAKIN' REPORTS, COLLABORATING DATA... BEING THE *SHIELD* AGENTS NICK *TRAINED* US TO BE.

SUDDENLY...

ERIC!

THE COUNCIL MUST BE FINISHED WITH HIM!

I ADVISE YOU NOT TO DISCUSS ANYTHING CONCERNING THE COUNCIL SESSION AMONG YOU. COMMANDER KOENIG HAS ALREADY BEEN SO ORDERED. I TRUST YOU UNDERSTAND.

JIMMY, YOU DON'T HAVE TO INFORM *US* ABOUT *SHIELD* POLICY!

BELOW, IN THE DEPTHS...

THIS SURE AIN'T WHAT YOU CALL THE *DIRECT ROUTE*, BUT I CAN'T AFFORD TO TAKE THE SAME WAY BACK TWICE. TOO *DANGEROUS*.

BUT I'VE BEEN WITHOUT *SLEEP* FOR TWO NIGHTS, AND IT'S STARTIN' TO *CATCH UP* TO ME.

CRUUNCH

WHAT'S THAT?

A *SHURIKEN*! GOTTA GET MY PISTOL!

FLIPFLIPFLIP

ARRGHH

SPLASH

ALL RIGHT. WHO'S UP THERE?

ONLY AN AGENT OF *SHIELD*, COLONEL...

...ABOUT TO PERFORM HER *SWORN DUTY*.

NO WAY, LADY. I KNOW *ALL* MY AGENTS BY SIGHT AND YOU AIN'T *ONE OF 'EM.*

THERE ARE MANY OF US YOU *DO NOT* KNOW, COLONEL. MORE THAN YOU CAN POSSIBLY IMAGINE.

YOU'RE FROM *ROXXON*, AREN'T YOU? YOU'RE FROM PROJECT DELTA!

VERY GOOD, OLD MAN. UNFORTUNATELY YOU WILL NOT LIVE TO DISCOVER ANYTHING MORE!

GOTTA *DUCK!*

FFZZATT AARRGH

NO GOOD. TOO TIRED. TOO SLOW!

YOU'RE FAST FOR AN OLD MAN.

FLIP

YEAH? YOU SHOULD SEE ME ON A *GOOD DAY.*

THWIP

NOW IT'S TIME WE TALKED...

... UNDERSTAND?

SP PUHN-LASH

NOW TELL ME HOW DID ROXXON INFILTRATE *SHIELD?* WHAT'S THE COUNCIL'S *GAME?* WHAT IS *DELTA?*

SHUT UP, FOOL!

THWOK

NOW YOU WILL DIE! AS THE COUNCIL HAS *ORDERED!*

WHOA! THAT WAS SOME HOOK. WHOEVER SHE IS, SHE'S *STRONG*, AND I'M TOO TIRED.

MEANWHILE, BELOW...

THAT TOOK ALMOST EVERYTHING I HAD... BUT *THAT* OUGHTTA PUT HER OUTTA COMMISSION FER AWHILE.

ARRGHHH

SMASH *SWOK*

UHHH

VERY *GOOD*, COLONEL, YOU'RE DOING VERY WELL. MUCH BETTER THAN THEY EXPECTED.

WHA--? HOW DID SHE RECOVER SO BLAMED FAST? AND HER STRENGTH... WHO IN SAM HILL IS SHE?

I SHALL REGRET CAUSING YOUR DEATH, COLONEL!

THWOK

I'M TOUCHED-- OOFF!

BUT FOR THE *GOOD* OF *SHIELD* YOU MUST *DIE*.

BLAM *ARRGGH*

SHE'S... *KILLIN'* ME... AN' THERE'S NOT A THING I CAN DO--

THAT PIPE... C'MON, NICK, GRAB IT...

USE IT!

AAAAAGGGG

SLAM

LADY, I'D LOVE... TA STAY AROUND... AN' CHAT... BUT I GOT THE FEELIN' I'D LIKE TA *LIVE* A LITTLE BIT LONGER.

NEVER THOUGHT I'D HIT A WOMAN LIKE THAT! BUT SHE'S NOT *DOWN* YET! I GOTTA FIND A PLACE TA *HIDE*... CATCH MY BREATH... SHEESH... I THINK I BROKE A COUPLE O' RIBS...

I GOTTA GET OUTTA HERE... GOTTA WARN THE AVENGERS... THE FF... SOMEBODY! I CAN'T LET HER--THEM--STOP ME! GOTTA PROTECT *SHIELD*. C'MON, FURY, THINK! YOU'RE SUPPOSED TO BE THE GREAT TACTICIAN!

NO SOUND FROM BIG RED. MAYBE I FINISHED HER *OFF?*

WISHFUL THINKIN'.

URRKK

FOOLISH MAN!

I TIRE OF THIS GAME, SO LET US END IT *NOW!*

SPLK-LASH

YOU ARE A THREAT TO *SHIELD* AND ITS GOALS, COLONEL, SO YOU MUST DIE!

AS A GOOD SOLDIER, I TRUST YOU UNDERSTAND. YOU REALLY HAVE NO *CHOICE*.

gurgle

NO! I AIN'T GONNA LET THAT HAPPEN!

URRRK

POW

I...I'M LOSIN' IT...MY LUNGS ARE BURSTIN'! BUT, IF I GIVE UP, NO ONE'S GONNA KNOW...ROLLINS AN' THE OTHERS WILL TAKE OVER...SHIELD WILL BE DESTROYED AN'...

SORRY, BABE, BUT NICK FURY DON'T DIE THAT EASY.'SPECIALLY WHEN SOMEONE'S RIPPIN' THE GUTS OUTTA MY ORGANIZATION. I AIN'T ALLOWIN' YOU OR ANYBODY ELSE TO DO THAT! GOT THAT?

SUCH BRAVADO, COLONEL. BUT YOU HAVEN'T BEEN PAYING ATTENTION. NO ONE IS DESTROYING SHIELD, WE ARE MERELY FULFILLING ITS DESTINY.

A DESTINY THAT NO LONGER INCLUDES YOU!

SNIKT

WHOA! SHE NICKED ME! ANOTHER INCH AN'... C'MON, NICK, STOP HER! IT'S NOW OR NEVER!

GOT YA! SORRY, HONEY, BUT I DON'T TAKE TOO KINDLY TO GETTIN' CUT!

THAT IS TOO BAD, OLD MAN! BECAUSE YOU CANNOT STOP ME. I AM FAR, FAR STRONGER THAN YOU. PITIFUL OLD FOOL!

SHE'S RIGHT, BLAST IT! SHE'S RIGHT!

...SEWHERE... COMMANDER **GABRIEL JONES**, WELCOME. YOU HAVE KNOWN COLONEL FURY FOR MANY YEARS. YOU SERVED TOGETHER IN THE FAMED HOWLER SQUAD IN THE SECOND WORLD WAR. INDEED, IT WAS COLONEL FURY WHO BROUGHT YOU INTO **SHIELD**. NOW HE STANDS ACCUSED OF TREASON...

SPARE ME THE BULL, SIRS...

LIKE YOU SAID I'VE KNOWN NICK A LONG TIME. AND I KNOW HE'S AN **HONEST** MAN. HE'D SOONER GIVE UP HIS RIGHT ARM THAN BETRAY **SHIELD** OR HIS COUNTRY.

COMMANDER **TIMOTHY DUGAN**, **SHIELD'S** SECOND IN COMMAND.

PERHAPS NO MAN HAS KNOWN NICK FURY LONGER OR AS WELL AS YOU. WITH THE EXCEPTION OF YESTERDAY'S UNFORTUNATE **INCIDENT**, YOU HAVE SERVED THIS ORGANIZATION IN A MANNER...

EXCUSE ME, SIRS...

OFFICER **JASPER SITWELL**.

YOU HAVE BEEN ON COLONEL FURY'S PERSONAL STAFF SINCE SHORTLY AFTER YOU JOINED **SHIELD**. YOUR BRILLIANT ANALYTICAL MIND HAS CREDITED THIS ORGANIZATION IN MANY SITUATIONS. YOU, PERHAPS, MORE THAN ANY OTHER AGENT, HAVE BEEN OFTEN NOTED FOR YOUR **LOYALTY** TO **SHIELD**.

HECK, AS FAR AS I'M CONCERNED NICK FURY *IS* *SHIELD.* HAS BEEN SINCE THE DAY I SIGNED ON.

AN INTERESTING POINT, JONES. BUT THE FACT REMAINS THAT COLONEL FURY HAS PLACED HIS COUNTRY, POSSIBLY THE ENTIRE FREE WORLD, IN GRAVE *JEOPARDY.* AS A LOYAL AGENT OF *SHIELD* WOULD YOU *TERMINATE HIS LIFE* IF SO ORDERED?

NOT UNLESS YOU CONVINCED ME NICK WAS *GUILTY*-- AND, FRIENDS, THAT'S GONNA TAKE A *LOT* OF CONVINCIN'. WHAT ARE YOU HIDING? WHY DON'T YOU SHOW YOUR...

THANK YOU, COMMANDER, THAT WILL BE ALL.

...BUT I WOULD LIKE AN EXPLANATION. WHAT'S GOIN' ON AROUND HERE? WHAT HAS NICK *DONE?* HAS IT GOT TO DO WITH THE *POWER CORE?*

SURELY YOU KNOW THAT THE COUNCIL OF DIRECTORS WORKS FOR THE *GREATER GOOD* OF *SHIELD.* IF WE CHOOSE *NOT* TO REVEAL CERTAIN ASPECTS OF THIS CASE, REST ASSURED THERE IS A GOOD REASON.

NOW, COMMANDER, WOULD YOU BE ABLE TO EXECUTE OR ORDER THE *EXECUTION* OF NICHOLAS FURY IF THE COUNCIL SO ORDERED?

SIRS, NICK FURY HAS BEEN MY FRIEND FOR MORE YEARS THAN I CAN COUNT-- AND *NO*, NO MATTER *WHAT* HE'S DONE, I COULDN'T DO THAT. NO, SIR, I'D RATHER KILL *MYSELF.*

IT IS A LOYALTY INSTILLED IN ME BY *COLONEL FURY*, SIRS. HE TRAINED ME, HE TAUGHT ME THE IMPORTANCE OF THIS ORGANIZATION IN KEEPING THE FREE WORLDS SAFE. EVERYTHING I *AM*, I *OWE* TO COLONEL FURY.

VERY COMMENDABLE, SITWELL, BUT COLONEL FURY IS NO LONGER THE MAN YOU *THOUGHT* HIM TO BE. HE HAS *CHANGED.* HIS ACTIONS THREATEN ALL OF *SHIELD.* INDEED, ALL OF THIS NATION IS THREATENED. IF SO ORDERED, WOULD YOU *KILL NICK FURY?*

I ...WAS *TAUGHT*...THAT A *SHIELD* AGENT SHOULD DO ANYTHING... *ANYTHING*... TO PROTECT THIS COUNTRY. I... I WOULDN'T BE THE AGENT NICK FURY *WANTED* ME TO BE IF I DIDN'T SAY... I'D HAVE NO CHOICE BUT TO *FOLLOW* THAT ORDER.

GOD FORGIVE ME.

YA GOTTA FIGHT, NICK! *SHIELD* DEPENDS ON IT... GABE, DUM DUM, *VAL*... MEBBE THE WHOLE BLAMED WORLD. YA CAN'T GET KILLED BEFORE YOU FIND OUT WHAT'S GOIN' ON...

SO C'MON, GET THAT BLASTED KNIFE! USE IT ON HER. THERE'S NO OTHER WAY!

KA-SHUNNK

I NEVER KILLED A *SHIELD* AGENT BEFORE. THAT'S SOMETHIN' ELSE I OWE THOSE LOWLIFES AT ROXXON. I FEEL SICK TO MY STOMACH...

MEBBE SHE'S STILL *ALIVE*... MEBBE I CAN SAVE HER... GET HER TO TALK...

MEBBE... I...

OH, LORD...

NICK, WHAT HAVE YOU GOTTEN YERSELF INTO?

AGENTS **ROLLINS** AND **WOO**, YOU HAVE PERFORMED ADMIRABLY. THE CHARADE IS NOW ENDED, AND THE DECISION MADE. DURING THE INTERROGATION SCENARIO, OUR FIVE SUBJECTS WERE BEING SECRETLY BIOSCANNED. BRAIN-WAVES, HEARTBEAT, PULSE RATE, EVEN SYNAPSE REACTION TIME WERE ALL BEING RECORDED AND THE DATA CORRELATED.

AS WE ANTICIPATED, ONLY **ONE** OF THE FIVE IS NOW SUITABLE. THAT CANDIDATE IS TO BE PREPARED FOR DELTA AS QUICKLY AS POSSIBLE. AS YOU KNOW, THE SAFETY OF **SHIELD** DEPENDS ON IT.

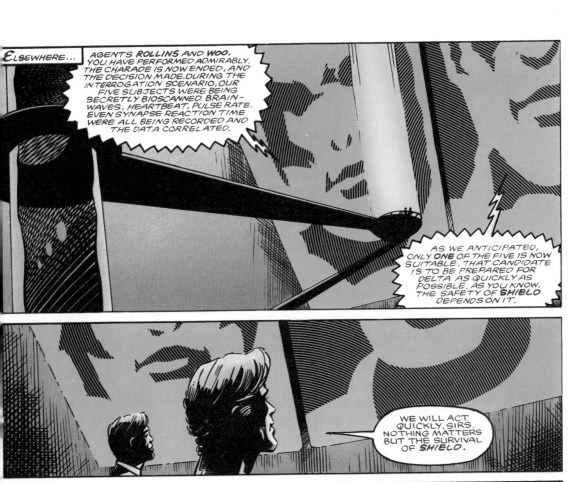

WE WILL ACT QUICKLY, SIRS. NOTHING MATTERS BUT THE SURVIVAL OF **SHIELD**.

LATER, AFTER THE COUNCIL HAS STOPPED TRANSMITTING FROM THEIR SECRET LOCALE...

WE HAVE JUST RECEIVED WORD THAT AGENT L-16'S LIFE SIGNALS HAVE TERMINATED.

FURY?

WHO **ELSE?** SHE WAS ASSIGNED TO FIND HIM. A PITY. SHE WAS ONE OF OUR **BEST**.

ALL THE MORE REASON TO PROCEED QUICKLY. FURY MUST NOT BE ALLOWED TO INTERFERE WITH OUR PLANS.

HE CANNOT, FOR HE DOESN'T HAVE THE SLIGHTEST **IDEA** WHAT OUR PLAN IS!

AT ANY RATE, IT IS A MOOT POINT. SOON, COLONEL FURY'S LUCK WILL **RUN OUT**, AND HE WILL **DIE**. IT IS INEVITABLE.

MEANWHILE...

VAL'S BEEN SO *QUIET* SINCE SHE TALKED WITH THE COUNCIL. POOR KID! THIS WHOLE THING WITH NICK MUSTA HIT *HER* THE HARDEST!

VAL, YOU *OKAY?*

WHAT? OH, YES, DUM DUM, I'M *FINE.*

WHY DID I *HESITATE* WITH THE COUNCIL? THAT WAS THE MAN I *LOVE* THEY WERE TALKING ABOUT!

WHAT HAVE I *BECOME* IF I'M WILLING TO LET-- OH --

LADY AND GENTLEMEN, THE COUNCIL HAS REQUESTED THAT I INFORM YOU THAT COLONEL FURY HAS BEEN *REPLACED* AS EXECUTIVE DIRECTOR OF *SHIELD* AT THIS POINT IN TIME. A GENERAL ANNOUNCEMENT WILL BE ISSUED SHORTLY.

WELL, DUM DUM, IF ANYONE CAN LEAD US OUT OF THIS INSANITY, *YOU* CAN.

YES, SIR, CONGRATULATIONS... IF THAT DOESN'T SOUND TOO *GAUCHE* UNDER THESE CIRCUMSTANCES.

I'M SORRY. YOU HAVE ALL MISUNDERSTOOD. COMMANDER DUGAN WAS NOT CHOSEN FOR THE POSITION... FOR *HEALTH* REASONS. HIS HEART CONDITION. THE NEW DIRECTOR OF *SHIELD* IS...

JASPER SITWELL!

WHAT?!

LATER, BELOW

AIN'T MUCH FURTHER... I GOTTA GET SOME REST. I AIN'T GONNA DO ANYONE ANY GOOD IF I CASH IN MY CHIPS DOWN HERE... I CAN'T LET THAT HAPPEN.

THAT'S WHY I GOTTA RUN... I HAVE TA FIND OUT EXACTLY WHAT'S GOIN' ON AT *SHIELD* AND REPORT... SOME JOKE. REPORT TO WHO, NICK?

WHOA, GETTIN' DIZZY... ...LOOSIN' MY BAL...

IN THE DARK, WITH NO SOUND BUT THAT OF THE RUSHING WATER, THE SEWER RATS BECOME BOLD, FOR THEY SENSE THIS BROKEN MAN IS NO THREAT TO THEM.

SPLASH!

BUT WHEN THE SOUND OF ANOTHER WHO COMES WALKING THROUGH THE DARK IS HEARD, THE RATS SCURRY...

...FOR NICK FURY IS NO LONGER ALONE.

SHIELD HQ, THE FOLLOWING DAY.

WELL, *DUM DUM,* HERE HE COMES, *JASPER SITWELL,* DIRECTOR OF *SHIELD,* REPORTING IN FOR HIS FIRST DAY ON THE JOB.

YA SOUND BITTER, *GABE,* DON'T BE. THE BOARD WAS RIGHT TA PASS ME OVER FOR PROMOTION, WHAT WITH MY BUM TICKER. JASPER'S A GOOD KID. HE'LL HELP US FIND NICK AN' STRAIGHTEN OUT THIS WHOLE MESS. RIGHT, *VAL?*

ATTENTION! ATTENTION! CLEAR THE LANDING DECK! SHIELDCRAFT EAGLE ONE IS LANDING!

IF IT CAN BE STRAIGHTENED OUT, DUM DUM, SOMETIMES I HAVE MY DOUBTS.

AND SHORTLY, AS A HONOR GUARD ASSEMBLES BEFORE THE CRAFT...

DIRECTOR SITWELL IS DISEMBARKING. ALL PERSONNEL AT ATTENTION! THE DIRECTOR IS TO MAKE A SHORT STATEMENT.

MY FELLOW MEMBERS OF *SHIELD,* I TAKE THE REINS OF POWER TODAY AS OUR ORGANIZATION FACES A MOST DIFFICULT TIME. IN THE LAST SEVERAL DAYS A SERIES OF CATASTROPHES HAS BEFALLEN US THAT THREATENS NOT ONLY OUR INTEGRITY BUT OUR MORALE AS WELL.

FIRST, THE THEFT OF OUR POWER CORE BY *HYDRA* AND *AIM,* AN EVENT THAT MUST BE OUR TOP PRIORITY TO RECTIFY, FOR THE CORE'S DESTRUCTIVE POTENTIAL IN THOSE HANDS IS UNTHINKABLE. SECOND, THE DEATHS OF SEVERAL *SHIELD* AGENTS IN THAT HIJACKING, INCLUDING COMMANDER *CLAY QUARTERMAIN,* ONE OF OUR MOST DECORATED AGENTS. AND LASTLY, THE SHOCKING BETRAYAL OF COLONEL *NICHOLAS FURY,* WHOSE APPREHENSION IS VITAL TO NATIONAL SECURITY.

THE MEETING HALL OF THE BOARD OF DIRECTORS OF *SHIELD*.

SITWELL'S SPEECH WAS... INSPIRING. I THINK HE'LL DO WELL. WE DID NOT EXPECT TO REPLACE NICHOLAS IN SUCH A MANNER. STILL, LIFE IS MADE UP OF SUCH UNEXPECTED CHALLENGES. TELL ME, HOW GOES THE RECLAMATION OF OUR LATEST ACQUISITION?

THIS IS THE CRITICAL PERIOD, OF COURSE. THE NEXT FEW HOURS WILL TELL THE TALE. AS PROMISED, OUR SANCTIMONIUS ALLIES, THE ENCODERS HAVE CUT THE TIMING OF THE PROCESS FROM WEEKS TO A MATTER OF DAYS.

YES, UNDOUBTEDLY, *HE* WILL BE A VALUABLE ADDITION, POSSIBLY MORE SO THAN ROLLINS, DON'T YOU THINK?

OF COURSE. WE CONSTANTLY EVOLVE. ROLLINS, SITWELL, KOENIG... ALL SHOW MARKED IMPROVEMENT. BUT, BEFORE LONG OUR LATEST ADDITION WILL JOIN US... AND, GENTLEMEN, HE WILL ASTOUND YOU. HE IS PERFECTION ITSELF. YET... ALL WILL BE FOR NOTHING WITHOUT FURY!

WE CANNOT BE ASSURED OF COMPLETE SUCCESS WITH DELTA UNTIL THAT VITAL COMPONENT HAS BEEN INTEGRATED INTO THE PROCESS. I CANNOT STRESS THAT ENOUGH.

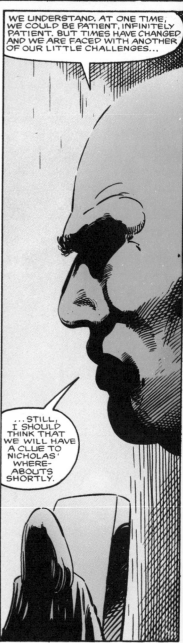

WE UNDERSTAND. AT ONE TIME, WE COULD BE PATIENT, INFINITELY PATIENT. BUT TIMES HAVE CHANGED AND WE ARE FACED WITH ANOTHER OF OUR LITTLE CHALLENGES...

...STILL, I SHOULD THINK THAT WE WILL HAVE A CLUE TO NICHOLAS' WHEREABOUTS SHORTLY.

"HELLO?"

"CAN YOU HEAR US?"

"WHA--?"

"I THINK HE'S COMIN' AROUND."

"I DO BELIEVE YOU'RE RIGHT."

"HUH?"

THERE YA GO.

WELCOME TO THE LAND OF THE LIVIN', SON.

L-LIVING?

NOW, NOW, DON'T TRY TO STAND UP JUST YET. YOU WUZ PRETTY BAD OFF WHEN I FOUND YOU. WHAT WUZ YOU DOIN' THAT FAR DOWN?

THAT'S NONE OF YOUR BUSINESS NOW, HAM. YOU KNOW THAT. LET THE POOR FELLA ALONE. HE LOOKS LIKE HE'S BEEN THROUGH ENOUGH WITHOUT YOU BADGERIN' HIM.

MARY'S RIGHT, HAM. THE GUY'S BEEN OUT NEARLY THE WHOLE DAY. GIVE HIM TIME TO WAKE UP, FOR PETE'S SAKE.

WHERE AM I?

THIS IS ME AND CHARLIE'S AND HAM'S PENTHOUSE APARTMENT, O' COURSE. AIN'T IT NICE? NOW TAKE SOME SOUP. THE BEST IN THE PLACE, I PROMISE YOU.

DON'T WORRY, YOU YOUNG FOLKS HEAL EASY ENUFF. WHY, I REMEMBER WHEN I WUZ YOUNG I DANCED WITH THE METROPOLITAN BALLET COMPANY.

THAT'D BE ABOUT THE TIME I TAUGHT THE CLASSICS AT OXFORD, EH? HEY, WHAT DID YOU DO ON THE OUTSIDE, YOUNG FELLA?

YOUNG? I AIN'T BEEN YOUNG IN A LONG TIME, FRIEND--

-- BUT UP 'TIL A FEW DAYS AGO, I WUZ THE DIRECTOR OF SHIELD.

SHIELD? THAT'S NICE, DEAR.

VERY GOOD, JASPER. NICHOLAS' ASSOCIATION WITH THE SO-CALLED SUPERHERO CONTINGENT HAS LONG CONCERNED US. NOW WHAT ABOUT FURY'S CLOSE ASSOCIATES AT *SHIELD* ITSELF?

THE THREE PRINCIPALS ARE BEING CLOSELY WATCHED BY OUR AGENTS.

"DUM DUM DUGAN'S NEIGHBORHOOD GROCER'S NEW CASHIER IS ONE OF OUR MEN. DUGAN CANNOT ORDER A HAM AND SWISS ON RYE WITHOUT A REPORT BEING FILED."

"GABE JONES CANNOT GO FOR A STROLL THROUGH THE PARK WITHOUT A FRIENDLY HOT DOG VENDOR OR A FEMALE PASSERBY KEEPING CLOSE TABS ON HIM."

"AND THE COUNTESS VALENTINA DE ALLEGRO IS ALSO UNDER OUR CONSTANT SURVEILLANCE."

I HOPE THE WEATHER CLEARS FOR CLAY'S FUNERAL TOMORROW. I CAN'T BELIEVE HE'S GONE. I CAN'T BELIEVE A LOT OF THINGS LATELY. EVERYTHING HAS FALLEN APART.

THE OTHER DAY THE BOARD ASKED ME IF I WOULD KILL NICK IF I WAS ORDERED TO DO SO... AND I COULDN'T SAY NO. I CAN'T GET THAT OUT OF MY MIND.

GOOD EVENING, COUNTESS. NASTY WEATHER, EH?

WHAT? OH, YES. DREADFUL.

YOU'RE THOROUGH, JASPER, I'LL GRANT YOU THAT. THAT MAILMAN, MY DOORMAN... BOTH *SHIELD* AGENTS, WATCHING ME MAKING SURE I DON'T MAKE A RUN FOR NICK.

THIS ISN'T THE LIFE YOU IMAGINED WHEN YOU WERE YOUNG, IS IT, VAL? NO, YOU WERE JUST ANOTHER JET SETTER ENJOYING ALL THAT WEALTH HAD TO OFFER. WHAT AN EMPTY FATUOUS LIFE IT WAS.

ISN'T THAT WHY YOU JOINED *SHIELD*? TO MAKE SOMETHING BETTER OF YOURSELF? TO HELP THE WORLD? AND NOW, IT HAS ALL COME TO ASHES.

AND YOU MADE ME THE PERFECT AGENT, DIDN'T YOU, NICK? LOYAL TO *SHIELD* ABOVE ALL ELSE. ABOVE EVEN YOU. AND NOW, I MAY HAVE TO KILL YOU, MY DARLING. AND I DON'T EVEN KNOW IF THAT IS WRONG.

OH, NICK, WHAT HAVE YOU DONE TO US? WHAT HAVE YOU DONE TO *ME*?

VERY GOOD, JASPER. YOU HAVE EFFECTIVELY CUT COLONEL FURY OFF FROM ANY POTENTIAL HELP. AND NOW, WE HAVE SOME NEWS FOR YOU: WE HAVE TRIANGULATED THE LOCATION WHERE AGENT 1-16'S LIFE-SIGNS TERMINATED: THE CATACOMBS BENEATH GRAND CENTRAL STATION.

IT IS REASONABLE TO ASSUME THAT FURY IS STILL HIDING OUT DOWN THERE. FIND HIM AND INITIATE OPERATION CLEAN OUT. WE CAN HAVE NO WITNESSES.

AS THE BOARD REQUESTS.

REMEMBER, JASPER, WE WOULD LIKE THE COLONEL TAKEN ALIVE, BUT IT IS NOT ABSOLUTELY NECESSARY. JUST MAKE CERTAIN WE RECOVER HIS BODY.

JASPER?

WOO. I DIDN'T SEE YOU IN THE SHADOWS.

I HAVE BEEN INFORMED. IT IS TO BE A TOTAL CLEAN OUT?

THOSE ARE THE BOARD'S ORDERS. WE HAVE NO CHOICE.

BELOW, IN THE DARK...

WELL, NICKIE, AND HOW ARE THE RIBS FEELIN' TODAY?

I DUNNO, MARY, YOU WRAPPED UP MY CHEST SO TIGHT, I CAN BARELY BREATH... BUT I THINK THEY'RE GONNA BE ALL RIGHT.

'COURSE THEY IS. MARY WUZ A NURSE AFTER SHE WUZ IN THE BALLET, AIN'T THAT RIGHT, MARY?

'COURSE IT IS. I WORKED WITH SCHWEITZER IN AFRICA. TAUGHT HIM EVERYTHING HE KNEW. HAVE SOME BOOZE, NICKIE. IT'LL KILL THE PAIN.

HERE COMES CHARLIE.

SWIPED US SOME FOOD FROM UP TOP. SORRY IT TOOK SO LONG, BUT THERE ARE A LOT OF NEW FOLKS DOWN HERE TONIGHT. FUNNY, 'CUZ IT AIN'T SO COLD OUT. GO FIGGER THAT OUT.

NEW FOLKS?

C'MON, NICKIE, I TOLD YA, IT'LL KILL THE PAIN.

NEW FOLKS?

OLD KENTUCKY
our mash sky
since 1979

SO -- YOU YOU *ARE* HERE AFTER ALL.

HOLD ON, HAM-- HOLD ON! I'LL GET YA *OUTTA* THIS. I *SWEAR* IT.

FZZATT

NICK...I...HURT SO...BAD...

I KNOW, PAL. *I KNOW.*

JUST...GOTTA...GET DOWN THIS *TUNNEL*... NO PROBLEM, HAM, YA HEAR?

FZZATT

NO GOOD, I'M OUTTA BREATH. I CAN'T OUTRUN THOSE *KIDS,* 'SPECIALLY CARRYING HAM.

SO I GOTTA MAKE SURE THEY CAN'T *CATCH* ME.

FZZATT

THE *IDIOT!* HE COULD HAVE BROUGHT THE WHOLE *TUNNEL* DOWN!

HE CUT US OFF! WE'LL NEED AN *EXCAVATION* TEAM.

I DON'T *UNDERSTAND*, COMMANDER. THE COLONEL HAD A CLEAR SHOT... WHY DIDN'T HE *KILL* YOU?

BECAUSE HE IS *WEAK*. HE STILL BELIEVES IN *FRIENDSHIP*.

"POOR FOOL. IT WILL PROVE HIS *UNDOING*."

HOLD ON, HAM. HOLD ON. WE'LL GET OUTTA THIS.

NICK... WHY?

WHAT KIND... OF PEOPLE WOULD DO... *SUCH THINGS?*

MY PEOPLE, HAM. HEAVEN HELP ME, MY PEOPLE.

LATER, SOMEWHERE IN THE DARK...

UGLY THING... LEAVIN' HAM'S BODY TO *ROT* IN THE DARK. TAKIN' HIS *COAT* FOR WARMTH...

BUT IT'S AN UGLY *WORLD*, AN' GETTIN' UGLIER EVERY SECOND... AN' THE *DEAD* DON'T NEED TO BE *WARM*.

I DON'T KNOW WHO I CAN *TRUST* ANY MORE... BUT YOU, *YOU* WOULD NEVER TURN AGAINST ME...

SWOOSH

BEEP BEEP BEEP

"COULD YOU?"

YES, DUM DUM. I'LL BE READY AT *TEN*. NO, CLAY'S BROTHER WON'T BE ABLE TO ATTEND. HE SOUNDED VERY *BITTER* WHEN I TALKED TO HIM.

I'M *FINE*. DON'T WORRY. I KNOW NICK WILL *CLEAR HIMSELF* AND WE'LL FIND OUT WHAT'S BEEN GOING ON. WE *HAVE* TO.

NOW, GET SOME *SLEEP*. TOMORROW'S GOING TO BE ROUGH ON *ALL* OF US.

CLK

BEEP BEEP BEEP

GOOD NIGHT, DUM DUM.

OH, LORD... *NICK!*

YOU MUST BE DESPERATE. I DON'T CARE HOW CLEVERLY THIS TRANSMITTER IS SHIELDED, SOMEONE COULD HAVE *SEEN* IT!

VAL, THERE'S NOT MUCH *TIME*. THESE THINGS DON'T STORE MUCH TAPE. LISTEN: THINGS AIN'T WHAT THEY SEEM. I NEED YOUR *HELP*, HON!

MEET ME AT OUR EAST RIVER MEETING PLACE AT 2300 HOURS TOMORROW. DON'T TRUST ANYONE! LOVE YA!

FZZIMM

CURSE YOU, NICK FURY!

ELSEWHERE...

THEN, HE HAS CONTACTED HER?

APPARENTLY, OUR SCANNERS PICKED UP SOMETHING, ALTHOUGH IT WAS DIFFICULT TO ESTABLISH ON OUR SCAN SWEEPS.

WE OBVIOUSLY CANNOT LET NICHOLAS ESCAPE AGAIN. SHOULD WE ORDER SITWELL TO INTERROGATE HER?

SUBTLETY HAS ALWAYS WORKED TO OUR ADVANTAGE. WE KNOW THE CONTESSA'S PSYCHOLOGICAL PROFILE. LET HER EMOTIONS WORK FOR US.

ON TO THE OTHER MATTER AT HAND, HOW GOES THE RECLAMATION?

AS PREDICTED, WITH OUR NEW SOURCE OF ENERGY, THE PROCESSING PERIOD HAS BEEN REDUCED BY 54.6 PER CENT. THE QUALITY OF THE PRODUCT HAS ASTONISHED US ALL. STILL, IT MAKES ONE LONG FOR THE FINAL COMPONENT. WE CANNOT WAIT ETERNALLY.

"NEVERTHELESS, TOMORROW SHOULD BE A *MOMENTOUS DAY* FOR US ALL."

AND NOW, THE DIRECTOR OF *SHIELD JASPER SITWELL* WOULD LIKE TO SAY A FEW WORDS.

I REALLY CANNOT *ADD* MUCH TO WHAT HAS ALREADY BEEN SAID HERE. BUT I THINK *CLAY QUARTERMAIN* WOULD LIKE TO BE REMEMBERED AS THE EPITOME OF WHAT A *SHIELD* AGENT IS. A MAN OF *INTEGRITY*, HE LOVED HIS COUNTRY, AND HE LOVED *SHIELD*.

HE BELIEVED IN WHAT WE STOOD FOR: THE RIGHTING OF *WRONG*, THE PROTECTION OF THE *WEAK*, AND MOST OF ALL, THE PRESERVATION OF *FREEDOM*. IN THE END, HE PAID THE *ULTIMATE PRICE* FOR LOYALTY: HE LOST HIS LIFE IN THE SERVICE OF HIS COUNTRY. WE WILL *MISS* YOU CLAY, AND WE WILL HONOR YOU BY HONORING *SHIELD*.

LOYALTY... INTEGRITY... *SHIELD*. HOW OFTEN HAVE I HEARD *NICK* LINK THOSE THREE SAME WORDS? AND NOW... I...

JASPER!

AHA! JUST AS WE ANTICIPATED!

MAY I *SPEAK* TO YOU FOR A MOMENT?

OF COURSE, COUNTESS. FOR YOU... ANYTHING!

ELSEWHERE...

I MUST ADMIT, I AM *IMPRESSED.* THIS IS VERY PROMISING. MY COMPLIMENTS TO THE *RECLAMATION CREW.*

HE'S STILL IN THE *MORPHEUS STATE,* IS HE NOT?

OF COURSE. WE FIND IT HELPS TO ALLEVIATE THE PSYCHOLOGICAL *TRAUMA.* YOU MAY SPEAK *FREELY* WITH HIM. HE'LL REMEMBER *NOTHING.*

VERY WELL. WE WERE SURPRISED THAT COLONEL FURY TURNED TO THE *CONTESSA.* OUR PROBABILITY STUDIES SUGGESTED THAT HE WOULD CONTACT EITHER *COMMANDER JONES* OR *DUGAN.*

NICK'S *CONFUSED* RIGHT NOW... MUCH AS HE'LL HATE TO ADMIT IT. HE HAD TO WEIGH HIS CHOICES; DUM DUM AND GABE ARE *OLD SOLDIERS* HE KNEW THEY'D FIND IT MUCH MORE DIFFICULT TO BETRAY *COMMAND.*

BUT VAL'S NEVER *HAD* MILITARY TRAINING. NICK HOPES THAT AND THEIR..."FRIENDSHIP" MAKES HER THE PERFECT CANDIDATE TO CONTACT HIM AND KEEP *QUIET.*

IT'S A SHAKY GAMBLE. ABOVE ALL ELSE, NICK INSTILLED A LOYALTY TO *SHIELD* TO HIS MEN.

INDEED, AND THAT HAS MADE THE COLONEL SO *USEFUL* TO US.

STILL, HE GAMBLES ON HUMAN RELATIONS. POOR MAN. HIS RELATIONSHIP WITH THE COUNTESS WAS *NEVER* AS STRONG AS EITHER OF THEM HOPED.

"WELCOME BACK, *COMMANDER QUARTERMAIN! SHIELD* HAS GREAT PLANS FOR YOU."

BACK? HAVE I BEEN *GONE?*

LOWER MANHATTAN...

RIB'S STILL RIPPIN' INTO MY GUT...FREEZIN' WEATHER AIN'T HELPIN'. HAM'S COAT AIN'T DOIN' MUCH GOOD.

C'MON, DON'T GO BEGRUDGIN' THE DEAD...*WHO KNOWS* YOU MIGHT BE JOININ' 'EM BEFORE THE NIGHT'S OVER.

SHE'S THERE.

VAL.

OH, NICK. YOU *CAME*.

I PRAYED YOU *WOULDN'T*.

I'M TAKING YOU BACK TO *SHIELD* CENTRAL.

AWW, HON, NOT YOU YOU...DON'T *YOU* TRUST ME?

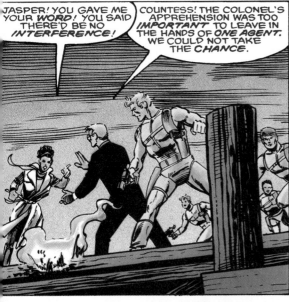

JASPER! YOU GAVE ME YOUR *WORD!* YOU SAID THERE'D BE NO *INTERFERENCE!*

COUNTESS! THE COLONEL'S APPREHENSION WAS TOO *IMPORTANT* TO LEAVE IN THE HANDS OF *ONE AGENT.* WE COULD NOT TAKE THE *CHANCE.*

APPREHEND? *ASSASSINATE* IS MORE LIKE IT! HE WAS *RIGHT!* YOU WANTED HIM *DEAD!*

VAL...

LET HER GO, MR. DIRECTOR. WE'LL DEAL WITH HER *LATER.* RIGHT NOW IT IS IMPERATIVE WE RECOVER THE COLONEL'S BODY.

YES. SO MUCH DEPENDS ON THE *DEAD,* DOESN'T IT?

AND, SOMEWHERE IN THE *DARK...*

...AND THIS JUST IN: THE NEW YORK CITY FIRE DEPARTMENT REPORTS THAT A METHANE GAS EXPLOSION IN THE TUNNELS BENEATH GRAND CENTRAL STATION HAS RESULTED IN THE DEATHS OF SEVERAL DOZEN HOMELESS...

...WHO HAD TAKEN REFUGE THERE FROM THE COLD. RESCUE TEAMS FOUND...

...NO SURVIVORS...

"*SHIELD* IS LIES, VAL...ALL LIES."

"*SHIELD, my pride an' joy. My army of good clean democratic soldiers . . . out there to save the world from the bad guys. What a joke. SHIELD ain't any o' those things. SHIELD KILLS.*"

chapter three: UNEASY ALLIES

NOT YET, ROLLINS!

NOT YET?! ARE YOU SERIOUS? THIS *RECOVERY* OPERATION IS TAKING ENTIRELY TOO LONG. DIRECTOR SITWELL WANTS CONFIRMATION IMMEDIATELY.

IT TOOK CAREFUL *PLANNING* TO LURE NICK FURY TO THIS PIER LAST NIGHT, GENTLEMEN...

"BUT THE COUNTESS REMEMBERED WHERE HER *LOYALTIES* LAY, AS AGENTS OF *SHIELD* MUST, AND REPORTED HER MIDNIGHT RENDEZVOUS WITH THE TURNCOAT."

"IT HAD BEEN DECIDED THAT THE COLONEL MUST BE SANCTIONED. A DECISION WE, OF COURSE, SPARED TELLING THE COUNTESS."

"HE'D CONTACTED HIS LOVER, THE *COUNTESS VALENTINE de ALLEGRO*, HOPING, NO DOUBT, TO ENLIST HER IN HIS QUEST AGAINST *SHIELD*.*"

*SUPREME HEADQUARTERS INTERNATIONAL ESPIONAGE LAW-ENFORCEMENT DIVISION.

NEVERTHELESS, WE MUST MAKE SURE FURY IS INDEED *DEAD*. ALIVE, HE REPRESENTS TOO GREAT A THREAT TO NATIONAL *SECURITY*.

THUS THE BODY MUST BE RECOVERED! IF I DISCOVER THAT YOU TWO OLD MEN HAVE BEEN *HAMPERING* THIS INVESTIGATION, I'LL HAVE YOUR HEADS!

NOW YOU JUST *HOLD ON* THERE, ROLLINS...

... I'VE BEEN KEEPIN' MY TEMPER UP TILL NOW... BUT DON'T GO ACCUSIN' ME AN' GABE OF ANYTHING! WE'RE NICK'S OLDEST *FRIENDS*! DON'T YOU THINK *WE* WANNA KNOW IF HE'S ALIVE OR NOT?

EASY, BUDDY! YOUR HEART...!

ANOTHER *OUTBURST* LIKE THAT, DUGAN, AND YOU MAY END UP IN THE BRIG!

YOUR ORDERS ARE SPECIFIC-- *RECOVER THE BODY OF NICHOLAS FURY!*

JONES, I WANT TO THANK YOU FOR RESTRAINING DUGAN. A SCUFFLE BETWEEN TWO HIGH LEVEL AGENTS WOULD NOT LOOK *PROPER* IN FRONT OF THE RANK AND FILE. YOU BEHAVED QUITE... ADMIRABLY.

DON'T SWEET TALK ME, MISTER. FOR SOME REASON, YOU HATE *ME* AND ANYBODY WHO *KNEW* NICK FURY. I'M NOT GOING TO LET YOU GOAD US INTO ANY INSUBORDINATE ACTION.

WE MAY BE OLDER THAN YOU NEWCOMERS, BUT WE'RE NOT *FOOLS.* YOU WANT TO PLAY *GAMES?* FINE. JUST REMEMBER WE HOWLERS DON'T GO DOWN EASY.

AN IMPRESSIVE SPEECH, JONES, BUT I THINK YOU AND YOUR FRIENDS SHOULD REMEMBER THAT *SHIELD* IS NOT A *REST HOME FOR OLD SOLDIERS.* YOU ARE EXPECTED TO OBEY ORDERS. GOOD DAY.

THAT OBNOXIOUS LITTLE--! HE WAS IN DIAPERS WHEN WE WERE STARTIN' *SHIELD!*

YEAH, AND I HAVE A FEELING THINGS HAVE CHANGED, DUM DUM. I'VE GOT THE FEELING THAT SOMETHING BIG IS GOING ON... BIGGER THAN NICK, BIGGER THAN THE POWER CORE--AND WE BETTER FIND OUT WHAT IT IS.

"SOMEHOW I THINK OUR *LIVES* MAY DEPEND ON IT."

SO, AGENT QUARTERMAIN, IN *YOUR* OPINION, IS NICK FURY DEAD?

BEATS ME. IF YOU GUYS DON'T FIND HIM *SOON,* I WOULDN'T LAY *MONEY* ON IT.

NICK'S ALWAYS BEEN TOUGH TO KILL. ISN'T THAT WHY YOU *HIRED* HIM?

THANK YOU. REPORT BACK TO REHABILITATION. YOU ARE TO BE *TRANSFERRED* SOON.

HIS *RETURN* WILL BE THE MOST DIFFICULT. HIS *DEMISE* WAS WIDELY KNOWN.

BUT WHAT A PRIZE HE IS! HE GIVES HOPE TO *THE PROJECT!*

THE SECTION OF MANHATTAN KNOWN AS SOHO, EARLY THE NEXT MORNING...

FOR MORE YEARS THAN HE CARES TO REMEMBER, ALEXANDER GOODWIN PIERCE HAS GOTTEN UP EVERY SUNDAY MORNING TO GET HIS FRESH DANISH AND THE SUNDAY TIMES.

BY MOST ACCOUNTS, HE IS A NONDESCRIPT LITTLE MAN, WHO PAYS HIS BILLS ON TIME, WORKS HARD ON HIS JOB, AND IS KIND TO ANIMALS.

ALEXANDER GOODWIN PIERCE PRIDES HIMSELF ON HIS REPUTATION. BECAUSE, LONG AGO, HE WAS SOMETHING VERY DIFFERENT...

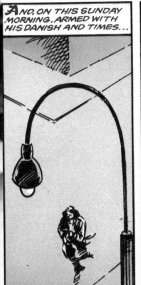

AND, ON THIS SUNDAY MORNING, ARMED WITH HIS DANISH AND TIMES...

...HIS PAST IS GOING TO CATCH UP WITH HIM.

MMMPFHHH

STAY NICE AN' QUIET, GOT IT?

YOU GONNA HELP ME... UNDERSTAND?

O-OF COURSE.

GOOD. 'CUZ IF YOU DON'T, I SWEAR... I MAY KILL YOU.

FOR NICK FURY HAS RE-ENTERED THE LIFE OF ALEXANDER GOODWIN PIERCE.

DOWNTOWN, THERE IS AN OFFICE BUILDING. FROM THE OUTSIDE, IT LOOKS LIKE ANY OTHER. BUT THIS BUILDING HOUSES THE HEADQUARTERS OF *SHIELD.*

*D*EEP IN THE LOWER LEVELS, LIES ONE OF *SHIELD'S* MOST MYSTERIOUS SECTIONS: THE *EXTRA SENSORY PERCEPTION DIVISION.*

LEVEL ·128

ES PD

*S*OME JOKINGLY CALL IT THE BRAIN WAVE GANG. BUT THEY DON'T KNOW WHAT GOES ON DOWN HERE. IT IS HARDLY A JOKE.

YOU GUYS GOT HERE QUICK. BUT THEN, YOU'RE GETTING *USED* TO THIS.

OUR SCANNERS CONFIRMED HE REACHED THE *THRESHOLD.* WE'LL TAKE HIM AWAY, LIKE THE OTHERS.

I DON'T THINK I CAN STAND SEEING THIS HAPPEN AGAIN.

YOU WILL. THEY KNEW THE RISKS. ACCEPT IT... THEY WERE *EAGER* TO SERVE *SHIELD...* AS ARE WE *ALL.*

I DON'T KNOW IF *ANYTHING* IS WORTH BECOMING A CATATONIC VEGETABLE FOR...

SHOULDN'T GO AROUND *SAYING* THINGS LIKE *THAT, ALLEN. COULD* GET YOU IN TROUBLE.

YOU WILL ENTER AGENT PSI-112'S *TERMINATION* RIGHT AWAY. RECORDS LIKE IMMEDIATE NOTIFICATION.

SURE -- EVERYTHING WILL BE NOTED, LIKE ALWAYS. WOULDN'T WANT TO KEEP RECORDS *WAITING.*

ESP DIVISION. AGENT *JOHN ALLEN,* DIVISION CHIEF REPORTING TERMINATION OF PSI-112. REQUEST NOTIFICATION OF NEXT TO KIN. WE NEED A REPLACE-MENT. WE ARE NOT OPERATING AT PEAK EFFICIENCY.

REPORT ACKNOWLEDGED, DIVISION CHIEF.

DIVISION CHIEF, BULL! I HOUSE SIT A ROOM FULL OF *ZOMBIES* WAITING FOR THE DAY THEY DIE. NICK FURY ORDERED THE *ESPERS* TO BE USED AT MAXIMUM RANGE. I TOLD HIM NO BRAIN COULD *ENDURE* THAT KIND OF PUNISHMENT, BUT HE *DIDN'T CARE!*

BUT HE'S TURNED *TRAITOR* NOW! MAYBE *JASPER SITWELL* WILL LISTEN TO REASON. MAYBE *HE* WILL STOP ALL THESE DEATHS.

AND, IN THE OFFICES OF THE NEWLY APPOINTED **DIRECTOR OF SHIELD...**

MR. STANE, I MUST SAY WE ARE GREATLY PLEASED THAT YOUR SHIPMENT OF LAZ-WEAPONRY HAS ARRIVED AHEAD OF SCHEDULE.

THANK YOU, MR. SITWELL, AT **STANE INTERNATIONAL**, WE PRIDE OURSELVES ON **EFFICIENCY**.

AS WE DO AT **SHIELD**.

I LOOK FORWARD TO A FRUITFUL ASSOCIATION, MR. SITWELL. I CAN ASSURE YOU THAT WE WILL DO OUR **UTMOST** TO MEET OUR COMMITMENTS TO **SHIELD**.

HAVING STANE IS A HAPPY CIRCUMSTANCE, JASPER. IT WAS EXTREMELY LUCKY THAT WE HAD **AGENTS** STATIONED AT STANE'S WHEN HE MET HIS... **FATE**. HIS TIMETABLE SUGGESTS THAT HE IS DUE AT THE **SPA** SOON, THOUGH.

YES, HE DID SEEM TO NEED SOME **REST**. SPEAKING OF OUR LOST SOULS, WHEN IS **CLAY** RETURNING? I HEAR HE'S MOST IMPRESSIVE.

HE'S BEING MOVED BY ROLLINS SHORTLY. FOR OBVIOUS REASONS, HE WON'T BE **JOINING** US FOR A FEW WEEKS. BY THEN, IT IS HOPED THAT HIS RETURN WILL NOT HAVE TO BE JUSTIFIED. FEW OF THE **ELITE** REMAIN.

AND NICK'S BODY?

NO **WORD** YET. WE MADE AN ERROR AMBUSHING HIM NEAR **WATER**. HIS **BODY** IS TOO IMPORTANT TO... EH?

WOO, OLD BOY, YOU ARE TOO **GRIM**!

SORRY TO INTERRUPT, BUT I'D LIKE TO HAVE A FEW **WORDS** WITH YOU AND OL' JASPER!

NOW, I KNOW YOU HIGH TECH SCI-FI TYPES ARE REAL *BUSY*, BUT OL' *AL MacKENZIE* JUST WANTS TO TALK ABOUT THE *FURY AFFAIR*. MY BOSSES BACK AT THE COMPANY ARE REAL *INTERESTED*... CONSIDERIN' HOW NICKIE GAVE THEM THE BEST YEARS OF HIS LIFE.

MR. MacKENZIE, YOU MAY BE OUR *LIAISON* WITH THE... COMPANY, BUT THAT DOES NOT MEAN THAT *SHIELD* IS REQUIRED TO DIVULGE OUR *SECRETS* TO YOU. COLONEL FURY IS *OUR* AFFAIR. AND IT IS MUCH TOO *COMPLEX* A SITUATION FOR YOUR ORGANIZATION TO COMPREHEND.

OH, JASP, THAT *HURT*. BUT YOU'RE RIGHT. US *PEDESTRIAN FOLKS* DON'T UNDERSTAND HOW YOU COULD LOSE A DIRECTOR AND A TOP SECRET POWER SOURCE IN TWO DAYS.

YOU FOLKS *DID* LOSE THE POWER CORE, DIDN'T YOU?

HOW DID YOU HEAR ABOUT *THAT*, MacKENZIE?

THE POWER CORE IS A CLASSIFIED *SHIELD* PROJECT. YOUR PEOPLE COULD NOT HAVE LEARNED ABOUT IT ON THEIR OWN.

IF THERE IS A *LEAK* IN *SHIELD*, WE'LL FIND IT, MacKENZIE. AS FOR *YOU*, CONSIDER YOUR LIAISON POSITION *TERMINATED*. OUR TWO ORGANIZATIONS HAVE *NOTHING* IN COMMON. DESPITE WHAT SOME POLITICIANS WOULD BELIEVE. JIMMY, SEE HIM *OUT*.

WITH PLEASURE.

YOU KNOW, YOU *SHIELD* GUYS ARE ALWAYS LORDING IT OVER THE REST OF US PLAYING STAR WARS. WELL, THE WORD IS YOU REALLY *BOTCHED* THIS ONE UP.

WHO KNOWS? YOU COULD LOSE YOUR *FUNDING* AND IT COULDN'T HAPPEN TO A *NICER BUNCH!*

ELSEWHERE... I HAVE THE FIRST AID KIT, SIR.

OK, BRING IT OVER HERE, NICE 'N SLOW.

REALLY, SIR, THERE'S NO NEED TO HOLD THAT GUN ON ME.

MAYBE SO, MAYBE NO.

I DON'T UNDERSTAND. I'VE ALWAYS BEEN LOYAL. YOU CAN TRUST--

PIERCE, I DON'T TRUST ANYONE.

I USED TO. THAT WAS MY MISTAKE.

SIR?

I TRUSTED IN A THING CALLED *SHIELD*, PIERCE. TRUSTED IN THE PEOPLE I WORKED FOR AND THE PEOPLE THAT WORKED FOR ME.

"AND WHAT DID IT GET ME? A DEAD FRIEND... BETRAYAL... AN AMBUSH... A SLAUGHTER O' INNOCENTS.

"*SHIELD*, MY PRIDE AN' JOY. MY ARMY OF GOOD CLEAN DEMOCRATIC SOLDIERS...OUT THERE TO SAVE THE WORLD FROM THE BAD GUYS.

"WHAT A JOKE, PIERCE, CUZ *SHIELD* AIN'T ANY O' THOSE THINGS. *SHIELD* KILLS.

IT KILLS, AND IT ENJOYS IT! IT SLAUGHTERS HELPLESS OLD PEOPLE. IT SHOOTS THEM IN THE BACK LIKE NAZI *STORMTROOPERS!* AND THEY'RE *MY MEN! MINE!*

COLONEL, I--

D'YA UNDERSTAND, PIERCE? I SPENT *YEARS* BUILDIN' THAT ORGANIZATION. I WAS *PROUD* OF IT! BUT IT WAS A *LIE!* ALL OF IT!

A DIRTY, STINKIN' FILTHY SCUMMY *LIE!*

ARE *YOU* IN ON IT, TOO? ARE *YOU* ONE OF THEM?

NAH. YOU'RE TOO *LOW-LEVEL.* A FLIPPIN' SLEEPER AGENT... PRACTICALLY A *CIVILIAN.* THEY WOULDN'T *TOUCH* YOU... *YET.*

THEY? COLONEL, WHO ARE *"THEY"?* YOU'RE TALKING IN *RIDDLES.*

IT DON'T MATTER, PIERCE. YA LOOK LIKE YOU WENT *SOFT* AS A SLEEPER. WE'LL HAVE TO GET THROUGH THE *FLAB* TO FIND THE *MAN...* BUT WE WILL. WE *HAVE* TO.

Y'SEE, AS OF NOW, YOU'RE A *RENEGADE* WITH ME. AND WE'RE GONNA START *FIGHTIN' BACK.*

AN' YOU'RE GONNA BE MY RIGHT HAND MAN. I'M REDUCED TO *THAT.*

"AN' IF I SEE THE SLIGHTEST SIGN YOU'RE *ONE* OF THEM, I'LL *KILL* YOU."

BEAUTIFUL WOMAN WHOEVER YOU ARE. IN A FEW MONTHS, YOU'LL BE AN *EMPTY HUSK.*

DID YOU PLAN A *CAREER* IN *SHIELD,* SLEEPING BEAUTY? A *FAMILY* MAYBE? JOKE'S ON YOU. NICK FURY TOOK THAT ALL AWAY WHEN HE ASSIGNED YOU TO THE *ESPER* SQUAD.

HE WANTED THE *ESPERS* TO SCAN *SHIELD* FOR ANY EVIDENCE OF *PSYCHIC ATTACK* OR *MASSIVE BRAINWASHING.* THE SECURITY OF THE ORGANIZATION IS AT STAKE. DOES *SHIELD* MEAN THAT MUCH TO YOU, FURY, THAT INNOCENTS DIE?

WHEN THEY *FIND* YOU, I HOPE THEY SKIN YOU *ALIVE.*

I CAN'T *WATCH* THIS ANY MORE!

I WANT TO SEE *WHY* PEOPLE ARE DYING. I'M UNDER ORDERS NOT TO SCAN THE *ESPER* DATA, BUT TO BLAZES WITH FURY! I'LL SEE WHY!

DATA MAT 17

LOOK AT THIS: *EVERY AGENT* CONTINUOUSLY SCANNED. *THOUSANDS* OF THEM... THEIR LIVING *BRAIN WAVES* RECORDED FOR REFERENCE.

DO YOU REMEMBER ANY OF YOUR *TRAINING*? HOW COULD YOU POSSIBLY DISCUSS *SHIELD* MATTERS IN FRONT OF AN *OUTSIDER*? ARE YOU *MAD*?

I'M *SORRY*, COMMANDER WOO, BUT I--

JIMMY, THESE ARE DIFFICULT TIMES FOR ALL OF US. LAPSES CAN NOW BE EXPECTED, ALTHOUGH NOT APPRECIATED. AGENT ALLEN, PLEASE MAKE YOUR *REPORT*.

...THE FLAT SCANS ARE INEXPLICABLE. ABOUT 28 PER CENT OF *SHIELD* OPERATIVES ARE IMPERVIOUS TO *SCANNING*. THIS IS IN DIRECT *VIOLATION* OF CHARTER ORDER...

YES, YES, ALLEN, OF COURSE. YOUR REPORT ON COLONEL FURY'S ORDER IS SHOCKING. OBVIOUSLY HE WAS FAR MORE *CORRUPT* THAN WE BELIEVED.

AS FOR THE FLAT SCANS, I'M SORRY YOU WERE NOT *INFORMED*. WE HAVE BEEN INVESTIGATING FURY FOR SOME TIME NOW. WE THOUGHT IT PRUDENT TO *BLOCK* A CERTAIN PERCENTAGE OF OUR AGENTS FROM THE *ESPERS* IN ORDER TO CONDUCT OUR INVESTIGATION.

STILL, SIR, OVER A *QUARTER* OF THE ORGANIZATION? AND-- IS THAT WHY YOU AND COMMANDER WOO DO NOT REGISTER--

OF COURSE! WE WERE *LEADING* THE INVESTIGATION.

THIS ISN'T GOOD. WE SHOULD HAVE RECRUITED *ALLEN*... BUT HIS PERSONALITY WAS NOT SUITABLE FOR FIRST STAGE.

THANK YOU, AGENT ALLEN. THERE WILL BE A FULL STAFF MEETING TOMORROW AT 0800 HOURS. BE PREPARED TO MAKE A *FORMAL REPORT* THEN.

I WILL, SIR. THANK YOU.

SLOPPY, JIMMY. THE FAKED FURY ORDER WAS *INDELICATE* TO SAY THE LEAST.

IT WAS ISSUED *BEFORE* EITHER OF OUR TIMES, BUT ALLEN--SURELY HE'LL CHECK THE RECORDS, NOTE COMMON *PERSONALITY TRAITS* AMONG THE FLAT LINE AGENTS--

JIMMY, IS YOUR *AGE* SHOWING? REMAIN CALM. AGENT ALLEN WILL BE *DEAD* BY THE END OF THE DAY.

ON LEVEL 102 OF SHIELD CENTRAL...

OH, HELLO, GAIL.

VAL!

I'M GLAD I RAN INTO YOU. I HAVEN'T HAD A CHANCE TO TELL YOU I'M SORRY ABOUT NICK AND THE AMBUSH. IT MUST HAVE BEEN--

HARD ON ME? BECAUSE I BETRAYED THE MAN I--A... FRIEND? NICK IS WANTED BY SHIELD! WHAT ELSE WAS I EXPECTED TO DO?

I DID MY DUTY. ISN'T THAT JUST THAT WHAT WE'RE ALL SUPPOSED TO DO?

WHOA.

SOMEWHERE OVER THE CENTRAL UNITED STATES...

ARE YOU COMFORTABLE, CLAY? WE DID EXPERIENCE SOME PRETTY ROUGH TURBULENCE A WHILE BACK.

GEEZ, ROLLINS, I'VE HANDLED WORSE THINGS THAN A BUMPY FLIGHT IN MY TIME. YOU'RE ACTING LIKE I'M ABOUT TO FALL APART OR SOMETHING.

JUST CONCERNED. YOU LOOK A LITTLE TIRED.

WELL, IF YOU HAVE TO KNOW, "DOC", I'VE HAD SOME PRETTY WEIRD NIGHTMARES LATELY.

NIGHTMARES?

YEAH. I SEE... FLAMES... ALL AROUND ME LIKE I'M ON FIRE AND THEN I WAKE UP WITH MY HEAD POUNDING. BIZARRE, EH?

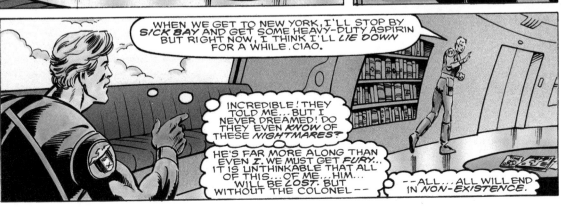

WHEN WE GET TO NEW YORK, I'LL STOP BY SICK BAY AND GET SOME HEAVY-DUTY ASPIRIN BUT RIGHT NOW, I THINK I'LL LIE DOWN FOR A WHILE. CIAO.

INCREDIBLE! THEY TOLD ME... BUT I NEVER DREAMED! DO THEY EVEN KNOW OF THESE NIGHTMARES?

HE'S FAR MORE ALONG THAN EVEN I. WE MUST GET FURY... IT IS UNTHINKABLE THAT ALL OF THIS... OF ME... HIM... WILL BE LOST. BUT WITHOUT THE COLONEL --

--ALL... ALL WILL END IN NON-EXISTENCE.

PHILADELPHIA, PENNSYLVANIA.

NICE *U TURN* YOU MADE BACK THERE, PIERCE.

I'M SORRY, SIR. I DIDN'T KNOW IT WAS A *ONE-WAY STREET.*

YEAH. FROM NOW ON, *I* DRIVE.

SIR, MY DUTIES NEVER INCLUDED VEHICULAR TRAFFIC. I'M A WHIZ AT DECODING CLASS A *HYDRA DISPATCHES...*

KNOPF & LILLICRAP INSURANCE AGENTS

CAN IT, PIERCE.

YE-ES? SIT DOWN, PLEASE. I'LL BE RIGHT *WITH* YOU.

CAN YOU *BELIEVE* THIS ARCHAIC DEVICE? I MEAN, RAH-LY, I REQUISITIONED A WORD PROCESSOR MONTHS AGO! I CANNOT BELIEVE THAT--

--I'M REDUCED TO THIS--

OH, RAH-LY, SIR!

CUT THE *ACT,* BABE. YOU KNOW WHO I AM. NOW TAKE ME *DOWNSTAIRS.*

DOWNSTAIRS? RAH-LY, SIR! WHAT WOULD YOU WANT WITH THE *BOILER?*

IT WORKS FITFULLY AT BEST. I FREEZE IN WINTER, I ASSURE YOU-- AIEEE!

PTOW

NOT NICE, SWEETHEART. I KNOW THE LOCATION OF YER *ALARM.* I KNOW *EVERYTHING* ABOUT THIS PLACE.

NOW OPEN UP THE *PASSAGE,* OR YOU CAN KISS YER WORD PROCESSOR *GOOD-BYE.*

LET'S SEE WHAT THE FOLKS BACK HOME HAVE TO SAY 'BOUT ME.

FURY, NICHOLAS JOSEPH. FORMER COLONEL, UNITED STATES ARMY. FORMER OPERATIVE. CENTRAL INTELLIGENCE AGENCY. FORMER PUBLIC DIRECTOR OF *SHIELD*, WANTED FOR TREASON, VIOLATION OF COUNCIL EDICT AND *SHIELD* CHARTER...

FZZZT

NOTHIN' TOO *SPECIFIC*. THEN, AGAIN, I DIDN'T DO ANYTHING 'CEPT FIND OUT TOO MUCH.

APPREHENSION IMPERATIVE, TERMINATION SANCTIONED. FORENSICS *SHIELD* CENTRAL ORDERS CONFISCATION OF FURY'S REMAINS.

NOW THAT'S INTERESTIN'...

"... THEY WANT MY *BODY*."

LISTEN... *PIERCE*, IS IT? WHY ARE YOU WITH HIM? FURY IS A TRAITOR TO *SHIELD*!

HE'S SETTING YOU UP! JOIN *US*... WE'RE ON THE SAME SIDE!

THE COLONEL IS NO TRAITOR. NOW, STAY BACK.

LET'S *TALK*. YOU'RE *SHIELD*. I'M *SHIELD*. YOU REALLY DON'T WANT TO DO--

THIS!!

THWAKK

÷AOOOWW...÷

FURY MUST BE DESPERATE TO TEAM UP WITH *FATTY ARBUCKLE* HERE.

HE MUST STILL BE DOWN *BELOW*.

GOOD, SEND OUT THE ALARM. COME ON... WE GET TO CAPTURE NICK FURY!

IF THAT DOESN'T GET ME TRANSFERRED OUT OF THIS DUMP, *NOTHING* WILL.

AND...

MEEP
MEEP

SOMETHING COMING IN OVER THE SHIELD PRIORITY FREQUENCY.

NICK FURY HAS ATTACKED SHIELD BASE TAU/CEI PHILADELPHIA. WE ARE ABOUT TO APPREHEND. HIS ACCOMPLICE IS IN CUSTODY.

HOLY--! BETTER REPORT TO COMMANDER ROLLINS!

COMMANDER--

I HEARD. I CAN'T BELIEVE MY STROKE OF LUCK. FURY MUST BE MAD TO ATTACK A SHIELD POST. HIS ARROGANCE IS ASTONISHING.

WE'RE TO ENGAGE IMMEDIATELY.

BUT, SIR, WE JUST CAN'T LAND IN DOWNTOWN PHILLY. ONLY SHIELD CENTRAL CAN AUTHORIZE SUCH A DEPARTURE FROM--

ROSS, THIS IS A PRIORITY ONE ORDER. DISOBEY AND I'LL MAKE SURE YOU END UP AT OUR DETENTION CENTER IN THE ALEUTIANS.

DO YOU UNDERSTAND?

UNDERSTOOD. ETA IN PHILADELPHIA: SIX MINUTES.

GOOD.

"LET'S HOPE THEY WON'T HAVE FURY BY THEN. I WANT TO TAKE HIM."

SMALL INSTALLATION... BUT *WELL-EQUIPPED.* BUILT WHEN *SHIELD* HAD A BLANK CHECK FROM CONGRESS. TWO PERSONNEL CARRIERS. EVEN THE MARK V IS A MODIFIED *PORSCHE.* NOT BAD.

FZZAMM

AWW... SHOOT!

BETTER GET MOVIN' BEFORE--

PIERCE, YOU *MORON!*

I MISSED! I NEVER MISSED AT THE ACADEMY!

I *MAJORED* IN EFFICIENT KILLING!

BETTER MEN THAN *YOU* HAVE TRIED TO KILL NICK FURY AND *FAILED!*

RAH-LY! WHAT DID *YOU* MAJOR IN, PIERCE? BROWN-NOSING?

ROSEN, FERNANDEZ, USE MR. CHEESE WHIZ AS A SHIELD...

FZAM

...FURY WON'T BE ABLE TO SHOOT AT *YOU* WITHOUT HITTING HIS *BUDDY.*

SHE'S GOOD. I'LL HAND HER THAT...

FZIIP

...TOO BAD I MAY HAVE TA *KILL* HER.

"IT'S A NICE LIFE, AIN'T IT, NICK?"

WHAT THE HECK *IS* THAT THING?

FASH

WOOM

HARD

FAN OUT! THEY REPORTED FURY WAS IN THE *LOWER LEVELS.* REMEMBER, FORENSICS WANTS HIS *BODY.* IT MUST--

QUARTERMAIN, WHAT DO YOU THINK *YOU'RE* DOING?

ARMING MYSELF, ROLLINS. ARE YOUR *EYES* GOING BAD?

YOU'RE *NON-COM* FOR THIS MISSION. COUNCIL ORDERS.

COUNCIL THIS! COUNCIL THAT! SINCE *WHEN* DO THEY TAKE NOTICE OF LITTLE *COGS* LIKE ME?

YOU'RE *HARDLY* A LITTLE COG, CLAY.

JUST STAY IN THE SHIP. *ALL RIGHT?*

NO, IT'S *NOT* ALL RIGHT, ROLLINS. I MAY BE IN THE *DARK* AROUND HERE, BUT IF NICK FURY'S TURNED *TRAITOR,* I WANT TO BE THERE WHEN THEY *ARREST* HIM. COUNCIL ORDERS OR NO.

BELOW... YER NOT BAD, GIRLIE, BUT YA LACK *SUBTLETY*...

...I DON'T HAVE TO SHOOT AT YER PALS. I CAN BLAST *BEHIND* 'EM...

FZZA-BAAM

...AND GET *ME* A HOSTAGE OF MY OWN.

FERNANDEZ, RIGHT? WELL, FERNANDEZ, I MAY HAVE TO BLAST YER *HEAD* OFF IF YER LADY FRIEND DOESN'T LET ME AND MY PAL GO.

YOU'RE *BLUFFING*, COLONEL.

I WOULDN'T LAY ODDS, SWEETHEART. IF YOU *WIN* THIS LITTLE STANDOFF, I'M A *DEAD MAN*. I GOT NOTHIN' TO *LOSE*... AND I *DON'T* INTEND TO DIE.

NOW, ON THE COUNT O' THREE. ONE...

...TWO...

KLIK

NEVILLE! HE ISN'T *JOKING*!

ALL RIGHT! YOU WIN. YOU'RE *EVERY* DIRTY LITTLE THING THEY *SAY* ABOUT YOU, COLONEL. WILLING TO KILL ONE OF YOUR *OWN*...

I'LL TAKE THAT. AND, MS. NEVILLE, AT THE ACADEMY I MAJORED IN INTEGRATED *CIVILIAN SURVEILLANCE*. I'M QUITE GOOD AT IT.

LET'S MOVE IT, PIERCE.

I DON'T CARE WHAT YOU'RE GOOD AT. YOU *STINK* AS A BACK-UP. YOU AN' ME GOTTA DISCUSS THE PRACTICE OF HOLDIN' *PRISONERS*.

YESSIR. I SHOULD NOTE THAT WHEN I WAS UP THERE, I THINK I HEARD--

--INCOMING
TROOPS.

FURY!
STOP!

FZZABAM

ROLLINS!

PIERCE,
WOULD YOU
MOVE?!?

OPEN
FIRE!

THIS CAR'S ARMORED LIKE A
TANK--GET BEHIND IT!

OMMPH!
YESSIR!

BLAMM

ROLLINS--YOU
DON'T HAVE TO
KILL HIM!

QUARTERMAIN!?
GET OUT OF HERE!

NICK! FOR THE LOVE OF HEAVEN, *GIVE UP!*

CLAY?

GET HIM TO THE *SHIP!* SUCH INDEPENDENCE CANNOT BE TOLERATED!

NICK!

SHUT HIM *UP!*

COLONEL! *QUICKLY!* THEY'RE DISTRACTED! GET IN THE *CAR!*

IT CAN'T BE.

FAZ

ARGGH!!

COMMANDER ROLLINS!

FORGET ABOUT *ME!* STOP THEM! STOP THEM!

FZZATT

FZZAATT

SCREECH

I'M SORRY FOR MY *INEPTITUDE* ON THIS MISSION, SIR. I THINK I'VE LEARNED A LOT.

WE'RE APPROACHING PROPER SPEED FOR *LAUNCH*, AREN'T WE, SIR?

THESE ESCAPE TUNNELS AVERAGE *THREE MILES*, DON'T THEY, SIR?

SIR?

GNU 558

NO SIGN OF PURSUIT. THOUGH AT THIS SPEED, IT IS *UNLIKELY*.

CLAY'S ALIVE.

SIR, IF YOU NOTICED, I LET YOU DO THE DRIVING.

SWWOSSHH

COMMANDER QUARTERMAIN IS BACK ON THE *SHIP*, SIR.

GOOD. WHERE ARE THE *LOCAL AGENTS?*

THERE, SIR. UNDER GUARD. ORDERS?

DISPOSE OF THE MEN, THEY'VE SEEN TOO MUCH.

BUT THE WOMAN, NEVILLE... I REMEMBER THE REPORT ON HER FROM THE *ESPER SQUAD*. SHE WAS TO BE RECRUITED WITHIN SIX MONTHS. A PERFECT CANDIDATE.

WE'LL SIMPLY SPEED UP THE PROCESS. SEND HER TO *DELTA*.

"WHAT WOULD WE DO WITHOUT THE ESPERS?"

MEETING TOMORROW WITH *SITWELL*. HAVE TO SIFT THROUGH THESE FILES--

WHAT--

HEY!

MR. ALLEN, THIS WAY, PLEASE.

WHAT'S GOING ON? YOU'RE *SHIELD*.

YES, AND YOU ARE A *DANGER* TO *SHIELD* AND MUST BE ELIMINATED.

OH, NO!

FRAK FRAK

LUCKY THING I DECIDED TO *TAIL* YOU.

YOU'RE THE GUY FROM *TODAY*! WHAT'S GOING ON? I KNOW THESE MEN! THIS IS *INSANE*!

RIGHT. A LOT OF THINGS TO DO WITH YOUR PALS SEEM CRAZY. I FIGURE A MAN THEY WANT TO KILL *CAN'T* BE ALL BAD. YOU'RE ONE. NICK FURY'S THE OTHER.

I CAN *PROTECT* YOU, ALLEN. AND I'M GOING TO FIND FURY. WANT TO TAG ALONG?

SHIELD CENTRAL, DAYS LATER...

YOU DISGUST ME.

I'M SORRY TO HEAR THAT, BUT A CHILD OFTEN HATES HIS *PARENT*.

YOU'RE AN *ABOMINATION*... A MEMORY BEST FORGOTTEN... AN EMBARRASSMENT OF THE PAST...

...A MASS OF SYNTHETIC AFFECTATIONS. YOU ARE ARTIFICE INCARNATE!

NO. I AM A LIFE MODEL DECOY.

A *LIFE* MODEL DECOY! NOW, THERE'S A MISNOMER... A *MOCKERY*! YOU KNOW *NOTHING* OF BEING ALIVE! OH, YOU MAY LOOK THE PART... BUT YOU HAVE NO LUNGS TO BREATHE... NO BLOOD PUMPS THROUGH YOUR VEINS.

YOU'RE NOTHING BUT A FORM MOLDED OUT OF PLASTIC...NO MORE ALIVE THAN A CHILD'S *BARBIE DOLL*.

WE ARE A *BIT* MORE COMPLEX... ALTHOUGH NONE OF US ARE *HUMAN*, ARE WE?

DON'T BE SARCASTIC! HUMANITY IS NOT FOR YOU, SO DON'T EVEN ATTEMPT THE PRETENSE OF *EQUALITY* WITH US!

PERHAPS YOUR PREJUDICES EXTEND *BEYOND* LMDS. PERHAPS THEY INCLUDE THOSE WHO ARE BEYOND THEIR FIRST GENERATION.

THERE ARE MORE OF *US* THAN YOU... AND WE WERE THERE AT THE *BEGINNING!* WE KNOW WHAT THE COUNCIL WANTS AND 'WE WILL OBEY THEM AS WE ALWAYS HAVE!

I MEANT NO *DISRESPECT.* IT'S JUST THAT THE TIMETABLE...

ROLLINS, DON'T YOU THINK *I*--EVEN MORE THAN YOU-- AM EAGER FOR FURY'S CAPTURE AND THE CULMINATION OF *DELTA?*

YOU SPEAK OF REDEMPTION! DO YOU KNOW HOW I *PRAY* FOR IT?

DO YOU BELIEVE THAT *JIMMY WOO* ENJOYS THE PROSPECT OF DYING-- *AGAIN?*

LOS ANGELES, CALIFORNIA.

A RECENTLY RE-OPENED DINER JUST OFF THE SANTA MONICA FREEWAY.

BIG JAKE'S DINER

CAFETERIA

MOTEL

I DON'T **GET** IT, **MOCKENZIE.** WHY ISN'T THE AGENCY BACKING YOU UP? WHY IS IT JUST THE **TWO** OF US ON HIS TRAIL?

BECAUSE BY CONGRESSIONAL MANDATE, **SHIELD** BUSINESS IS **SHIELD** BUSINESS. THERE'S ENOUGH JEALOUSY BETWEEN OUR TWO OUTFITS WITHOUT **US** PLAYING **WATCHDOG** FOR THE OTHER.

STILL, MY BUDDIES I'VE CONTACTED HAVE KEPT ME INFORMED OF SUSPECTED **SHIELD** INSTALLATION **BREAK-INS.** UNLESS I'M WRONG **NICK FURY** IS BEHIND THEM.

HAM AND EGGS, BOYS! EAT 'EM WHILE THEY'RE NICE AND GREASY.

I'M SURE **HE'S** THE KEY. HE MUST HAVE FOUND OUT SOMETHING THE BIG GUYS DIDN'T LIKE. LIKE YOUR DISCOVERY OF THE **FLAT BRAIN WAVE SCANS** OF A LARGE SEGMENT OF **SHIELD** OPERATIVES. THOUGH THAT DIDN'T SURPRISE ME.

AND TO THINK I BELIEVED **FURY** WAS THE **ROTTEN APPLE.** SITWELL AND WOO TRIED TO HAVE ME **KILLED.**

C'MON, ALLEN. YOU GUYS MIGHT GO AROUND IN BLACK TIGHTS... BUT YOU'RE STILL IN THE SPY BUSINESS. AND PEOPLE GET **KILLED** IN THE SPY BUSINESS. IT'S A **PREREQUISITE.**

AGENT L-14B...

WE'RE GOING IN FOR A **IDENTI-SCAN** NOW. PLEASE ADJUST FOCUS.

IDENTI-SCAN ENGAGED. WE SHOULD HAVE THE INFO IN ABOUT TEN SECONDS.

YEAH? WELL, HURRY UP. I THINK THE BLONDE ONE THINKS I'M COMING ON TO HIM!

DON'T WORRY. I HAVE IDENTI-SCAN CONFIRMATION. ALPHONSO MacKENZIE, CENTRAL INTELLIGENCE AGENCY LIAISON, ASSIGNMENT SHIELD, AND JOHN ADAMS ALLEN, LATE THE HEAD OF THE ESPER SQUAD.

EVERYTHING WORKED PERFECTLY. YOU MAY PROCEED, AGENT L-14B.

GEEZ, HERE SHE COMES AGAIN! HOW MANY CUPS OF COFFEE DOES SHE EXPECT A MAN TO DRINK?

IT MUST BE YOU, MacKENZIE. HAVEN'T YOU NOTICED HER STARING AT YOU?

IT'S PHEROMONES OR SOMETHING. WOMEN CAN'T RESIST MEEEE...

WHAT A PITY WE WON'T BE ABLE TO TEST THAT THEORY, MR. MacKENZIE. BUT IF YOU OR YOUR FRIEND MAKES A MOVE, I'LL VAPORIZE A BELOVED PART OF YOUR ANATOMY.

OUCH.

HOLLYWOOD, CALIFORNIA.

EVERYONE KNOWS THAT IT'S NOT ALL TINSELTOWN ANY MORE-- IF IT EVER WAS...

IN PLACES, IT HAS BECOME THE HABITAT OF JUNKIES, MUGGERS AND LADIES OF THE EVENING.

TONY STARK, THE INDUSTRIALIST, KNOWS THAT, AND HE REGRETS COMING HERE TONIGHT...FOR A VARIETY OF REASONS.

WHERE *IS* HE? I *KNEW* THIS WAS A MISTAKE... ESPECIALLY WHEN I HEARD IT WAS HERE IN THE SLEEZE ZONE.

HE MADE IT SOUND LIKE AN *ORDER*... HE ALWAYS DID. I KNOW HE'S IN TROUBLE. CAN'T SAY I'M REALLY *SORRY*.

HE SAID SOMETHING OF NATIONAL IMPORTANCE WAS ABOUT TO OCCUR. I ADMIT THAT PIQUED MY CURIOSITY...

...BUT HE'S *TEN MINUTES LATE.* HE'S NOT GOING TO SHOW, IF HE EVER REALLY--

--WAS!?

VIPP

WATCH IT! WHO THE HECK ARE YOU?

ALEXANDER GOODWIN PIERCE. I'M SORRY I WAS DELAYED. I COULDN'T PULL YOU THROUGH THE HOLOGRAM WHILE THERE WERE *PEOPLE* ABOUT.

THAT WALL WAS *SOLID.* I CHECKED.

ELEVATOR DOOR OPENS FOR FIVE SECONDS. IT IMMEDIATELY ENGAGES THE HOLOGRAM SO THE OPENING IS INDISCERNABLE.

INTERESTING. MY FIRM COULDN'T DO *BETTER.*

NOW, TELL ME, WHERE IS...

...NICK FURY?

EVENIN', STARK. LONG TIME NO SEE, HUH?

MAYBE. BUT THAT'S A SIN I'LL PAY FOR *LATER*. BUT FOR NOW, *SHIELD'S* GONE BAD. ROXXON'S INVOLVED...MAYBE *HYDRA*, *AIM*. I DUNNO. I NEED *HELP*, STARK...WITHOUT IT, THEY WIN.

...BUT I'VE NEVER LET MURDERERS...BUTCHERS...BEAT ME BEFORE. AND I'M NOT ABOUT TO NOW. SO YOU HELP ME, STARK, OR--

-- I SWEAR I'LL TELL THE WORLD THE TRUTH ABOUT *IRON MAN*...

...AND YOU.

I DON'T KNOW WHAT YOU'RE TALKING ABOUT, FURY. BUT I'M NOT *ABOUT* TO STAND HERE AND LISTEN TO YOUR VAGUE THREATS.

DOES HE *KNOW* I'M IRON MAN? HE DIDN'T A FEW MONTHS AGO. HOW COULD HE HAVE FOUND OUT?

I DON'T *WANT* TO DO IT, STARK. I RESPECT YOUR *PRIVACY*. BUT WHEN THE STAKES ARE THIS BIG, SOMETIMES YA GOTTA DO *UGLY THINGS*.

I AIN'T *LYIN'*, STARK, ABOUT *SHIELD*. WHY WON'T YOU *ACCEPT* THAT?

BECAUSE *SHIELD* IS BIG, FURY, ALMOST TOO BIG. IT'S *WORLDWIDE*. IF IT HAS GONE BAD, THE RAMIFICATIONS ARE MIND-BOGGLING.

I'LL THINK ABOUT WHAT YOU SAID. I'LL *CONTACT* YOU...

...AND I WON'T REPORT YOU.

I DIDN'T THINK YOU *WOULD*.

OKAY, PIERCE, WE'VE *HOOKED* HIM. NOW FOR PHASE TWO: WE KIDNAP A *SHIELD* FIELD COMMANDER.

YESSIR. OUR TAPS INTO *SHIELD* COMMUNICATIONS HAS REVEALED THAT A MAJOR *RENDEZVOUS* IS TO TAKE PLACE HERE SOON. THE FIELD COMMANDER WILL CERTAINLY HAVE TACTICAL KNOW--

PIERCE, BUTTON UP. Y'KNOW, I LIKED YOU BETTER AS AN *ACCOUNTANT*.

YESSIR.

THE HOLLYWOOD HILLS, SOME HOURS LATER...

IT IS A COLD NIGHT. BUT I BARELY FEEL THE STING. NERVE ENDINGS ARE DECAYING. SYNAPSES ARE FAILING. JUST LIKE *BEFORE*... AND BEFORE *THAT*...

...AND EACH TIME *SHORTER* THAN THE LAST. I DO NOT WISH TO LOSE ANY MORE OF MYSELF... NONE OF US DO. SO WE MAKE A PACT WITH THE *DEVIL* AND PRAY FOR *DELIVERANCE*.

IT IS ALL LIKE A *NIGHTMARE*... AND I CANNOT *WAKE UP*.

COMMANDER WOO, THE *SIGNAL*! SHE'S HERE... LORD HELP US.

YES, IF HE HEARS OUR PRAYERS.

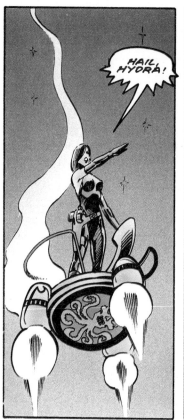

HAIL HYDRA!

YOU ARE *MADAME HYDRA*, I BELIEVE. THERE IS NO NEED FOR YOUR THEATRICS. WE ARE HERE TO INFORM YOU THAT THE *POWER CORE* WILL BE READY FOR TRANSPORT TOMORROW.

VERY GOOD. THE SUPREME HYDRA WILL BE PLEASED.

AND THE OTHER COMPONENT IN THE PLAN, OLD MAN?

WE KNOW HE IS IN *LOS ANGELES*, HE HAS BEEN GUIDED HERE THROUGH CAREFULLY LEAKED COMPUTER FILES.

WE ARE SMOKING HIM OUT *NOW*.

STARK ENTERPRISES, LOS ANGELES...

INCREDIBLE. FURY MEANS *BUSINESS.* I'M SURE OF THAT. WHAT COULD MAKE HIM SO *DESPERATE?* WHAT DOES HE FEAR *SHIELD* IS DOING--IF THEY'RE DOING ANYTHING AT ALL?

BUT IF *SHIELD IS* CORRUPT, THEY COULD EASILY DIVERT ATTENTION BY FALSIFYING RECORDS, TAMPERING WITH FILES...EVEN *FRAMING* SUSPICIOUS DIRECTORS?

DID I JUDGE FURY *GUILTY* BECAUSE OF SOMETHING HE CLAIMS NO KNOWLEDGE--EH?

EVENIN', STARK--

--LONG TIME NO SEE, HUH?

LMD FURY, ROLLINS, COMMAND CENTRAL: ENGAGE VISUAL SCAN.

VERY GOOD, ROBOT. NOW ENGAGE *SENSOR SCANS.* WE MUST TEST STARK TO SEE IF HE *KNOWS* ANYTHING, AND WE NEED *DATA* ON HIM. HE IS OWNER OF THE WORLD'S LARGEST *SPACE TECHNOLOGY* CORPORATION.

F-FURY.

WHAT ARE *YOU* DOING HERE? YOU'RE A *WANTED MAN.* SITWELL CONTACTED ME YESTERDAY.

STARK, I NEED YOUR *HELP.* I GOTTA GET OUT OF THE COUNTRY--

AND YOU CAME TO *ME!*?! ARE YOU *CRAZY*? I COULD END UP IN PRISON!

STARK'S READINGS INDICATE *AGITATION*-- THAT ISN'T SURPRISING. THE LMD HAS ACCOMPLISHED HIS PURPOSE. THE *REAL* FURY APPARENTLY HAS NOT BEEN IN TOUCH WITH STARK...

...AND WE HAVE THE PROPER PRELIMINARY READINGS ON STARK TO OPEN A DELTA PROGRAM ON HIM. HE WILL ONE DAY BE A VALUABLE *ADDITION* OUR CAUSE.

TERMINATE SESSION.

I WAS AN *IDIOT!* I THOUGHT I COULD *TRUST* YOU--

MY MISTAKE!

SOK

DON'T FOLLOW ME, AN' DON'T SEND YOUR BUDDY *IRON MAN* AFTER ME. HE WON'T FIND ME.

INCREDIBLE! THEY SENT AN *LMD!*

BUT WHY? WHAT DOES *SHIELD* WANT WITH *ME*?

SHIELDBASE, SOUTHERN CALIFORNIA SECTION, THIRTY-SIX MILES EAST OF LOS ANGELES.

AND THEY NEVER SUSPECTED THE DINER WAS A *SHIELD* LURE?

NO, *COMMANDER KOENIG.* AND THEY OFFERED NO RESISTANCE WHEN THEY FOUND OUT, ALTHOUGH THE *SEDATIVES* IN THEIR FOOD MAY HAVE HAD SOMETHING TO DO WITH THAT.

VERY GOOD. IT'S COMFORTING TO KNOW AGENT ALLEN ONLY ESCAPED HIS FATE FOR A MERE *TWO WEEKS.* ONE DOES NOT ESCAPE *SHIELD.* DISMISSED.

AYE, COMMANDER.

WELL, THAT'S A RELIEF. BAD ENOUGH WITH *FURY* OUT THERE. WE COULDN'T AFFORD *ANOTHER* LOOSE VARIABLE.

ALTHOUGH THEY WERE NEVER *TRULY* LOOSE. MACKENZIE AND ALLEN WERE TAILED FROM THE BEGINNING AND ALL OF MACKENZIE'S CALLS TO HIS FELLOWS WE RE-ROUTED TO *SHIELD VOICE SIMULATORS* WHICH FED THEM FALSE REPORTS GUIDING THEM HERE.

JIMMY?

WHA--FORGIVE ME. I AM LOST IN THOUGHT OFTEN LATELY. MY *TIME* IS *NEAR.*

BUT NOW I THINK IT IS TIME TO MEET OUR *GUESTS...*

"...THEY MUST BE *VERY CURIOUS*."

WHAT TH--! GOOD LORD, JIMMY! WHAT'S *HAPPENED* TO YOU!?

I'M AFRAID THAT IS NONE OF *YOUR* CONCERN, MR. MacKENZIE.

YEAH-- WELL IT'S THE *CIA'S* AND ONCE THEY FIND OUT WHAT YOU'VE DONE! KIDNAPING AN AGENT--

BUT THEY *WON'T*. THEY DID FIND VERY SENSITIVE DOCUMENTS IN YOUR APARTMENT-- PLUS OTHER EVIDENCE THAT YOU'VE BEEN A SOVIET AGENT FOR YEARS.

JUST ONE DAY AFTER YOU RESCUED MR. ALLEN, YOU WERE PLACED ON YOUR AGENCY'S *ELIMINATION LIST*. WE WERE VERY *EFFICIENT*. WE ALWAYS ARE.

YOU'RE *BLUFFING!*

I ASSURE YOU I AM *NOT*. YOU WILL BE KILLED ON SIGHT BY YOUR FELLOW AGENTS. BUT REST ASSURED, THEY WILL NEVER HAVE THE *CHANCE*.

AS FOR AGENT ALLEN, HE WAS NOT SCHEDULED TO BE *PROCESSED* FOR ANOTHER SIX MONTHS... BUT THEN HE STUMBLED ON THE *DELTA SCANS*.

PROCESSED? WHAT DO YOU MEAN?

BOTH MEN ARE CONSIDERED EXPENDABLE.

VARIABLES OFTEN ARE. *GUARDS!*

BAH-WOOM

AS EXPECTED, AN ATTACK IS REPORTED AT OUR LOS ANGELES BASE.

SO, NICHOLAS HAS TAKEN THE *BAIT*. WE CERTAINLY LEFT HIM ENOUGH *CLUES*.

OUR TIMETABLE WAS *SET BACK* SLIGHTLY WHEN NICHOLAS STUMBLED UPON DELTA. AN UNFORESEEN EVENT THAT IS EVEN NOW BEING *RECTIFIED*.

THOSE AGENTS STILL AT THE L.A. BASE ARE TO OFFER ONLY *MINIMAL RESISTANCE*. WOO, OF COURSE, MUST *ESCAPE* TO PLAY OUT HIS PART. KOENIG, I ASSUME, HAS BEEN PREPARED?

OUR SACRIFICIAL LAMB? YES, HE KNOWS WHAT TO DO. THE *IMPLANT* WILL BE ACTIVATED AT THE PROPER MOMENT...

"...POOR NICHOLAS WILL BE DRAWN DEEPER AND DEEPER INTO THE MYSTERY."

BLAMM

THE WALL!

IT'S *FURY!* HE'S COME!

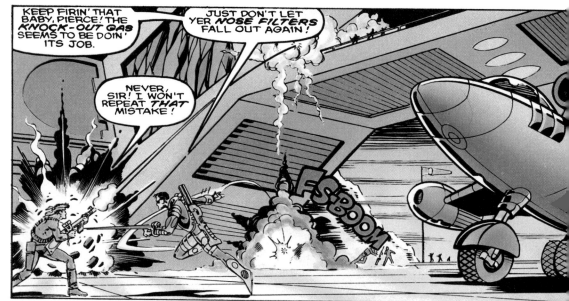

GAS 'EM ALL! I'M GOIN' *IN*.

THEY'RE FALLING LIKE *CHATTEL*, SIR!

SWELL.

THAT WAS MY LAST *STUN GRENADE*... LOOKS LIKE IT DID THE TRICK.

COLONEL FURY! WOO WENT OUT THE BACK PASSAGE!

PIERCE, I'M GOIN' AFTER WOO. COVER THESE GUYS...

...AND FOR PETE'S SAKE, WATCH YER *BACK*! EVERYONE OUTSIDE SHOULD BE OUT FOR HOURS, BUT YA NEVER CAN TELL.

SIR, I WISH YOU WOULDN'T ALWAYS REMIND ME OF MY *PAST MISTAKES*. I'M UP TO THE TASK.

THERE'S *JIMMY*. MUSTA BEEN AFFECTED BY THE GAS... HE'S MOVIN' SLOW.

WELL, MY MOTHER ALWAYS SAID, "NICK, DON'T LOOK A GIFT HORSE IN THE MOUTH--"

HOW YA DOIN'--

--JIMMY!?

NICK, YOU FOOL--

--I HAVE AN *APPOINTMENT* TO KEEP.

THWACK

STUPID! STUPID! ALMOST...CRUSHED... MY LARYNX...

...GOTTA CATCH...BREATH...

HE'S GETTIN' AWAY...WHY WAS HE HERE? AND...WHAT HAPPENED TO HIM?

FIRST, CLAY... *ALIVE*...NOW JIMMY AN *OLD MAN!* I DON'T GET IT.

SIR? COMMANDER WOO IS NOT WITH YOU?

NO, HE ISN'T, PIERCE. HE HAD A PRESSING ENGAGEMENT.

OH.

OKAY, SO I SCREWED UP THIS TIME. WHAT'S THE *SITUATION?*

THE BASE'S COMPLEMENT HAS EITHER FLED OR IS UNCONSCIOUS OUTSIDE. THE AREA SEEMS TO BE STRANGELY UNDERMANNED.

NOTICED THAT, DID YA? LIKE SOMEONE *WANTED* US TO GET THIS FAR.

AMONG OUR CAPTIVES ARE THESE TWO GENTLEMEN WHO WERE WOO'S *PRISONER'S*-- AL MacKENZIE, *CIA*, JOHN ALLEN, *ESPER* SQUAD.

I RECOGNIZE 'EM.

WE'VE MUCH TO DISCUSS, COLONEL.

I'M SURE WE DO.

BUT NOT HERE. WE'RE GOIN' SOME-PLACE *SAFE*, AND YOU'RE COMIN' *WITH* US, ERIC.

DO I HAVE MUCH *CHOICE?*

NONE AT ALL.

"IS THIS ANY WAY TO TREAT AN *OLD FRIEND*, NICK?"

"I DON'T KNOW *WHO* WHO MY FRIENDS ARE ANY MORE, ERIC."

BUT IF YOU'RE *STILL* ONE, I'M SORRY I HAVE TO DO THIS. IF YOU'RE NOT, I'M NOT GONNA SHED ANY TEARS.

NOW, WHAT DO YOU KNOW ABOUT ALLEN'S REPORT ON THE FLAT BRAIN WAVES ON THE *ESPER* SCREEN?

IS *SHIELD* BEING *MIND-CONTROLLED?*

WHAT MAKES YOU THINK *I* KNOW ANYTHING?

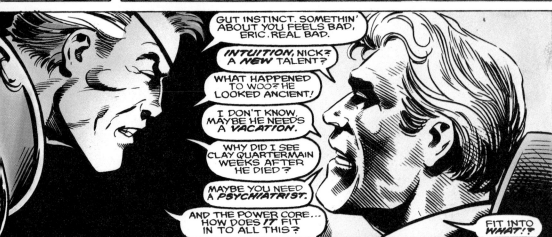

GUT INSTINCT. SOMETHIN' ABOUT YOU FEELS BAD, ERIC. REAL BAD.

INTUITION, NICK? A *NEW* TALENT?

WHAT HAPPENED TO WOO? HE LOOKED ANCIENT!

I DON'T KNOW. MAYBE HE NEEDS A *VACATION.*

WHY DID I SEE CLAY QUARTERMAIN WEEKS AFTER HE DIED?

MAYBE YOU NEED A *PSYCHIATRIST.*

AND THE POWER CORE... HOW DOES *IT* FIT IN TO ALL THIS?

FIT INTO *WHAT!?*

COLONEL, WOO MENTIONED SOMETHING ABOUT A *PROCESS.* IF WE FIND THAT, THE PUZZLE MIGHT BEGIN TO FALL INTO PLACE.

POSSIBLY--

--BUT I THINK YOU'LL NEED SOME *HELP.*

WHO!?

KILL THE LIGHTS. THIS DEVICE ILLUMINATES AN *LMD'S* ENERGY FIELD. NO MATTER *HOW* SOPHISTICATED THE ROBOT MIGHT BE, HUMANS REGISTER QUITE DIFFERENTLY.

HAVE FAITH, NICK.

YOU'RE SURE THAT THING'S GONNA *WORK?*

WE'RE ALL GLOWIN' THE SAME. GUESS OL' ERIC'S THE *REAL McCOY.* GUESS THEY ALL WERE. TOO BAD. I WAS KINDA HOPIN'...

NICK, YOU POOR *FOOL*... YOU HAVEN'T EVEN BEGUN TO GUESS THE TRUTH.

YOU WANTED TO KNOW WHERE WOO IS? HE IS AT THE DOCKS AND *YOU* CANNOT STOP HIM AND HE HAS YOUR PRECIOUS *POWER CORE.*

SN A P

KOENIG!

YOU INSULT US BY COMPARING US TO THOSE *THINGS!*

AR RG GH!

"IN THE END, WHAT ELSE *CAN* HE DO?"

WHERE IS THAT OLD FOOL? I DO NOT TRUST THESE *SHIELD* SHADOW MEN, BUT THE *SUPREME HYDRA* COMMANDS THAT I DO *BUSINESS* WITH THEM.

MADAME, HE IS HERE.

MY APOLOGIES, *MADAME HYDRA*. I AM USUALLY PROMPT, BUT I WAS DETAINED.

I WANT NO EXCUSES. WHERE IS THE *CORE*? THERE IS A CHILL IN THE AIR--AND I DO NOT LIKE THE *DAMP*.

WEEEEEEEE

I DO NOT FEEL THOSE THINGS... ANY MORE. BUT THE CORE COMES.

ORIGINALLY, THE CORE WAS A *DIVERSION* TO KEEP FURY FROM SUSPECTING THE *TRUTH* UNTIL IT WAS TOO LATE--

--NOW IT WILL SERVE AS A DIVERSION AGAIN TO SAVE US ALL.

YOU SPEAK IN *RIDDLES*, OLD MAN. *REDEMPTION* THROUGH THIS DEVICE? I THINK ALL OF YOU IN *SHIELD* ARE MAD.

PERHAPS. NOW TAKE IT. AND, ONE DAY, IF ALL GOES WELL, I WILL AGAIN FEEL THE CHILL AND THE DAMP.

"Aww, yer gettin' paranoid, Fury . . . there ain't nothin' to worry about – – 'cept gettin' killed."

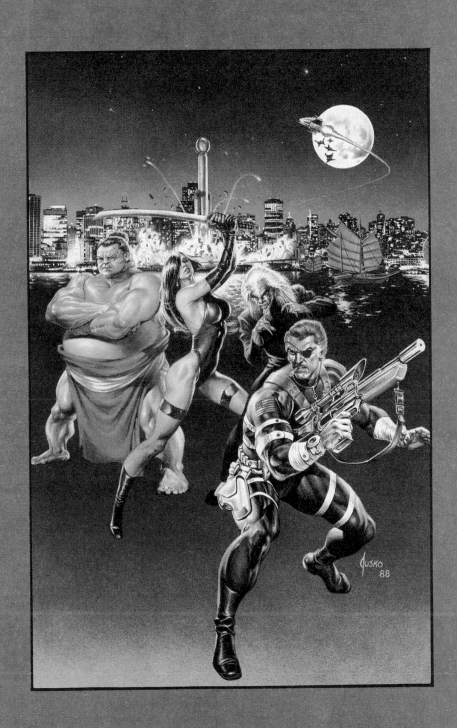

chapter four: **THE EASTERN CONNECTION**

SONY CORPORATE HEADQUARTERS, TOKYO, JAPAN.

YES, WE'VE BEEN GIVING YOUR PROPOSAL MUCH THOUGHT, AND WE ARE VERY INTERESTED.

I'LL BE TRAVELING TO THE STATES ON THE TWELFTH. MAKE THE ARRANGEMENTS, PLEASE, MISS YOSHIRO.

BMW, MUNICH, WEST GERMANY.

AFTER CAREFUL STUDY, WE'RE SATISFIED YOUR PROPOSAL HAS ASTOUNDING PROFIT POTENTIAL FOR BOTH OUR COMPANIES... SEE YOU ON THE TWELFTH.

I SHOULD BE GONE A WEEK OR SO. I WANT SCHMIDT AND WOLFF FROM R AND D TO ACCOMPANY ME.

ATT, NEW YORK, USA.

NO PROBLEM! THE TWELFTH IT IS! WE'RE DEFINITELY EXCITED! THIS'LL SHAKE UP THE BOYS ON WALL STREET, EH?

ROXXON'S NEW TELECOMMUNICATIONS PLAN COULD MEAN BILLIONS. I WANT OUR BEST MEN IN ON THIS.

IMPERIAL CHEMICAL INDUSTRIES, SYDNEY AUSTRALIA.

THIS REPRESENTS AN EXCITING DEVELOPMENT IN PETROCHEMICAL RESEARCH! WE WERE LOOKING INTO THAT AREA OURSELVES. THE TWELFTH, THEN!

MEMO TO THE BOARD, MS. WILLIAMS. ROXXON PROPOSES A JOINT RESEARCH VENTURE... A PROJECT THEY'VE NICKNAMED DELTA!

AND IN ALL THE WORLD, ONLY ONE MAN POSSESSES THE *PANACEA* WE SO DESPERATELY NEED. AND HE IS THE ONE MAN WHO SEEKS TO DESTROY US--*NICK FURY.*

HOW *SIMPLE* THINGS WOULD HAVE REMAINED IF YOU HAD NOT DISCOVERED THE *SHIELD-DELTA-ROXXON* CONNECTION AND REPORTED IT TO FURY.

I WAS *UNINITIATE* THEN, AS WERE *YOU!* BESIDES, FURY WILL BE IN OUR HANDS SOON AND ALL WILL BE *WELL!*

HE FOLLOWS THE POWER CORE TO *HONG KONG,* EXACTLY WHERE THE BOARD DESIRES HIM.

AND IF THE BOARD IS *WRONG?* EACH DELAY BRINGS US CLOSER TO *REGENERATION.*

NO! THEY WILL HAVE HIM *BEFORE* OUR TIME COMES! I'VE SEEN THE TIMETABLE!

TIMETABLES...PROJECTIONS...REPORTS... THE SOUL OF OUR ORGANIZATION, JACK. CHARTS AND GRAPHS... I ALWAYS HAD FAITH IN THEM. SO DID *YOU...*

BUT PEOPLE LIKE NICK, GABE...THEY BELIEVED IN *FATE* AND *CHANCE.* WHO WILL WIN IN THE END, I WONDER?

BLASPHEMY, MR. DIRECTOR?

WAIT...SOMEONE ENTERS THE CHAMBER.

IT'S *WOO.* HE WAS SCHEDULED TO FINISH *REGENERATION* TODAY. HE LOOKS-- DIFFERENT.

OF COURSE, JACK! THIS IS HIS *FIFTH* GENERATION. CHANGES ARE TO BE EXPECTED.

HIS EYES! HIS EYES LOOK DEAD! HE LOOKS LIKE THEM...A LIVING MANNEQUIN! I WON'T *ACCEPT* THAT!

LOST FAITH IN YOUR TIMETABLES SO QUICKLY, JACK? BY THE WAY, HAVE YOU NOTICED? YOU'RE GOING *GRAY?*

I WAS INSTRUCTED TO COME HERE. YOU WERE MY *COMRADE CELL?*

YES, JIMMY. CAN'T YOU REMEMBER US? TRY!

EASY, JACK. MEMORIES... PERSONALITY FADE. DON'T BE AFRAID OF HIM. HE'S A REMINDER OF OUR PRECARIOUS *MORTALITY.* OUR BEACON OF DESPAIR...

UNTIL *FURY* IS DELIVERED.

SPUNKLASH

THERE. THAT'S THE TUB.

EASY, BOYS. GOTTA MAKE SURE THIS AIN'T A--

--TRAP.

SO, NICK FURY, YOU HAVE FINALLY *ARRIVED*.

SOMEWHERE ELSE...

THE CORE IS SECURED. AND NICHOLAS?

ANTHONY STARK LOANED HIM A *QUINJET*. HE SHOULD BE ARRIVING ANYTIME NOW.

IT ALL MOVES TOWARD FRUITION. NICHOLAS HAS TAKEN THE BAIT SO TANTALIZINGLY OFFERED TO HIM BY *ERIC KOENIG'S* DEATH. I AM DELIGHTED.

IT IS ALMOST *FRIGHTENING* TO CONCEIVE THAT WE ARE *SO CLOSE*. THERE WERE TIMES... WHEN THE UNEXPECTED HAPPENED... THAT I FEARED ALL WOULD BE *UNDONE*.

I *ENJOY* THE UNEXPECTED. THE MECHANICS OF SURPRISE KEEPS LIFE FROM STAGNATING. I DO BELIEVE I WOULD NOT HAVE ENJOYED OUR VICTORY *HALF* AS MUCH HAD NOT NICHOLAS STUMBLED ONTO OUR PLAN.

HE STILL KNOWS SO *LITTLE*. SOON, OUR POLICING AGENT WILL BE SECURED, AND OUR ECONOMIC OBJECTIVES BEGUN.

BREATH-TAKING, ISN'T IT?

VERY...

PERHAPS WE SHOULD *RE-FORM*, MY DEAR? WE HAVEN'T SINCE THE FURY MELODRAMA BEGAN.

I'LL CHECK THE GENETIC TABLES TO FIND SOMETHING SUITABLE. WE'LL CELEBRATE IN *STYLE*, MY LOVE.

AS IS OUR DUE, MY HEART. FOR SOON WE SEND OUT...

...THE ASCENSION CELL!

NEW JERSEY...

ROXXON. PLACE STINKS. ALWAYS HAS, ALWAYS WILL.

WE'VE HAD SOME *RUN-INS* WITH THEM OVER THE YEARS AND BEFORE EVERYTHING WENT CRAZY, NICK WANTED A *FULL REPORT* ON THOSE JOKERS.

BUT, *VAL*, I TELL YA, LOOKIN' FOR A CLUE THERE IS LIKE LOOKIN' FOR THE PROVERBIAL NEEDLE IN THE HAYSTACK.

IT'S THE *ONLY CHANCE* WE HAVE, *DUM DUM*. WE HAVE TO CLEAR NICK...PROVE HE'S INNOCENT.

YEAH, BUT *HOW?* TO DO THAT, WE GOTTA GO AGAINST THE *BOARD*... AND NOT EVEN *NICK* COULD DO THAT.

MAYBE BECAUSE HE WAS TAKEN BY SURPRISE. WE HAVE THE LUXURY OF KNOWING THE BOARD SEEMS TO BE *INVOLVED*. WHY ARE YOU RELUCTANT? ARE YOU *AFRAID?*

I'M JUST SAYIN' WE'RE UP AGAINST SOME PRETTY *TOUGH ODDS*, MISSY. AND WE'D BE PRETTY *STUPID* NOT TO BE AFRAID OF THE BOARD.

DUM DUM'S RIGHT, VAL. WE DON'T EVEN KNOW WHO THE BOARD *IS*.

AT LEAST *YOU'RE* TALKIN' SENSE, GABE.

VAL'S RIGHT, TOO, DUM DUM. *ROXXON* MAY BE THE KEY TO THIS AFFAIR. AND WE HAVE TO INVESTIGATE, BUT THE BOARD MUST NEVER *SUSPECT*.

SO DUM DUM AND I WILL HANDLE ROXXON.

GABE!

VAL, TO HELP NICK WE HAVE TO PLAY THE FAITHFUL *SHIELD* AGENT. ALWAYS OBEYING ORDERS. AND YOU GOT NEW ONES THIS MORNING, DIRECT FROM OUR BELOVED *BOSSES*.

YOU'RE BEING REASSIGNED... TO A DIVISION CODENAMED *DELTA*.

HONG KONG.

NICE SET UP, PAIL. YEARS BEEN GOOD TO YOU.

THEY SAY LIVING WELL IS THE BEST REVENGE, NICHOLAS.

WE USED TA THINK JUST *LIVIN'* WAS REWARD ENOUGH BACK WHEN WE DEALT WITH THE RED CHINESE.

THOSE WERE EXCITING TIMES. YOU CALLED IT "LIVING ON THE EDGE." A TIME OF EXCITEMENT, WHEN ONE'S BLOOD RAN THROUGH THE VEINS LIKE QUICKSILVER.

I REMEMBER JUST A LOT OF *BLOOD*. PERIOD.

NOW, BEFORE WE START SINGIN' "AULD LANGE SYNE", WHAT ABOUT *THIS* JOKER? CAN HE BE TRUSTED?

NICK, THAT "JOKER" IS MY *SON*.

AND IN THIS DANGEROUS VENTURE YOU PROPOSE I WOULD TRUST *NO ONE ELSE.*

CALL ME THE NEW KID ON THE BLOCK, BUT IF FURY FOUGHT IN WW II AND KOREA...HOW COME HE LOOKS SO *YOUNG?*

YOU SCI-FI BOYS REALLY *WORRY* ME SOMETIMES, PIERCE. YOU REALLY DO.

I DUNNO, MAC. GUESS WE ALWAYS CHALKED IT UP TO *CLEAN LIVING.*

LATE THAT NIGHT...

YOU'VE COME! GOOD, GOOD!

IS SHE WAITING?

OF COURSE, OF COURSE! SHE WILL *ALWAYS* WAIT FOR HER BELOVED.

HE'LL CONTACT US AT *SUNSET*?

IS HE PREPPED?

YES, ONCE WENG ASCERTAINS HIS CONTACTS TRULY KNOW THE LOCATION OF THE *HYDRA* BASE, HE WILL SIGNAL US.

PULSE IS STEADY.

PAIL, YOU AN' ME GO WAY BACK. YOU WERE ONE O' THE *BEST*. ARE YOU SURE YOU CAN *HANDLE* THIS?

ARE YOU CONCERNED FOR MY HEALTH, NICK, OR DO YOU FEAR I WILL RUIN YOUR *PLAN*?

WE BEGIN THE *INCISION*.

YOU ARE WRONG. I WAS *THE* BEST. I SERVED MY GOVERNMENT TO THE FULLEST. NOW, IN MY OLD AGE, I AM EXPECTED TO LIVE OUT MY DAYS PLACIDLY. FORGOTTEN, DECAYING, VEGETATING.

PAIL, IT AIN'T *THAT* BAD.

NOW THE *IMPLANT*.

ISN'T IT?

WHEN *YOU* ARE OLD, NICK-- ALTHOUGH EACH PASSING YEAR THAT APPEARS LESS LIKELY-- YOU CAN COME AND TALK TO ME. AS FOR NOW... I GO WITH YOU TONIGHT.

AND NOW FOR THE *SECOND* COMPONENT OF OUR PLAN.

THIS DON'T FIGURE, GABE. I *REMEMBER* THE DELTA PROPOSAL...

IT WAS DESIGNED TO RETRAIN SELECT AGENTS TO CARRY OUT MISSIONS WITH *EXTREME PREJUDICE.* SUPPOSED TO FREE 'EM OF THE *GUILT FEELINGS* OR SOMETHING.

AND THE BOARD IS ASSIGNING *ME* THERE? *WHY?* WHAT DO THEY WANT?

VAL, THIS IS ALL NEW TO *ME,* TOO, OKAY?

BUT NICK *KAYOED* IT. SAID IT SOUNDED LIKE *BRAINWASHIN'* TO HIM. I THOUGHT THAT WAS *THAT.*

IF WE ACCESS THIS FILE MAYBE WE CAN FIND SOMETHING OUT.

ACCESS CODE SH-DIA

PROJ DELT

WELL, IT LOOKS LIKE THE BOARD OVERRULED NICK IN A BIG WAY.

BUT THAT'S *IMPOSSIBLE!* HOW COULD WE *NOT* KNOW?

THERE ARE *THOUSANDS* OF *SHIELD* AGENTS LISTED HERE. AND *ALL* OF THEM HAVE BEEN ASSIGNED TO DELTA.

WHAT'S MORE-- WHY IS THE BOARD LETTIN' US FIND OUT *NOW?*

IT'S LIKE THEY'RE PLAYIN' A *GAME*... TELLIN' US WE AIN'T A *THREAT* SO IT DON'T MATTER IF WE FIND OUT A LITTLE. SEE IF YOU CAN FIND OUT MORE, GABE... LOCATIONS, SPECIFICS.

NO CAN DO. LOOKS LIKE THE BOARD ONLY WANTS TO GIVE US A *GLIMPSE.*

I DID NOTICE A CURIOUS REPETITION OF SOME OF THE EARLIER DELTA AGENTS. *WOO'S* BEEN BACK FIVE TIMES.

DATA HOLD 1A

AND JASPER AND ROLLINS WERE BOTH ASSIGNED THERE RECENTLY.

THE TERRIBLE TRIO? THIS HAS GOT TO BE CONNECTED TO *NICK.* BUT, GABE, THIS IS TOO *FISHY*... VAL CAN'T GO!

I CAN TAKE CARE OF *MYSELF*, MR. DUGAN.

AND IF THIS DELTA ASSIGNMENT CAN HELP US FIND OUT WHAT'S BEEN GOING ON... THEN *I'M GOING.*

AND WE'D *BETTER* FIND OUT, BOYS, BECAUSE I THINK IT'S *MORE* THAN NICK NOW. I THINK *ALL* OUR NECKS ARE IN THE NOOSE.

AH, GAMES WITHIN GAMES.

POOR MADAME HYDRA, YOU WILL SURELY BE *REWARDED*...

...TO YOUR *HEAVENLY REWARD.*

TERMINATE SUPREME HYDRA SIMULATION.

THE COUNCIL GROWS *EXCITED*, MY LOVE. THEY FEEL THE VICTORY WITHIN THEIR GRASP.

AND SO IT IS. FURY CHASES HIS PRECIOUS *POWER CORE* LIKE DON QUIXOTE AFTER HIS *WINDMILLS*. THE CORPORATE INVITATIONS HAVE SNAGGED OUR EAGER VICTIMS. OUR *SHIELD* LOYALISTS FAITHFULLY ACT OUT OUR MACHINATIONS. SOON, ALL WILL BE HERE... AND OUR DREAMS COMPLETED.

YES.

YOU LOOK VERY *STRUCKER-LIKE*, MY LOVE.

WELL, HE WAS ONE OF THE *PROGENITORS*.

AND YOU? A MIXTURE OF de FONTAINE, RUNCITER, AND BROWN, I BELIEVE?

OF COURSE!

THE *WOMEN* IN FURY'S LIFE. I THOUGHT YOU'D APPRECIATE THE *JEST*.

ROXXON RESEARCH CENTER...

DEEP IN ITS DEPTH LIES A COMPLEX CODE NAMED DELTA.

STOP IT! BLAST YOU, STOP IT!

I DO NOT UNDERSTAND, CANDIDATE NEVILLE. YOU HAVE BEEN CHOSEN.

SUBJECT'S RESPIRATION UP 12.3 PER CENT. HEART RATE ACCELERATED 18.92 PER CENT. SUGGEST TERMINATE ENCODING PROCESS.

AGREED, COMPUTER.

WHY DO YOU *RESIST* THE SACRAMENT OF ENCODING? IF YOU DO NOT RECEIVE IT, YOU WILL BE DENIED THE GIFT OF *REPEATED LIFE!*

THE ALL-KNOWING COUNCIL HAS DEEMED YOU *WORTHY.* IF--

ENCODER.

IT DOES *NOT GO WELL?*

NO, LAURA BROWN. HER STRENGTH OF WILL IS *REMARKABLE.*

THE NEW CANDIDATES WILL BE MUCH MORE *RESISTANT* THAN THOSE THE *ESPER*s CHOSE AS THE FIRST DELTITES.

A *NEW COMPLEMENT* IS ARRIVING. PREPARE THEM AND THOSE ALREADY HERE FOR TRANSPORT. FURY IS EXPECTED AT THE PRIME LOCATION SOON.

THE *ASCENSION CALL!* AT LAST, THE DELIVERER IS IN OUR HANDS.

NOT *YET,* ENCODER, BUT SOON. VERY SOON.

SO...FURY... THE TRAITOR... IS *BEHIND* ALL THIS...

I SWEAR... I'LL MAKE HIM PAY!

FOR BLOOD IS THE SACRED TINCTURE -- THE ESSENCE OF THE LIFEFORCE ITSELF!

FORGIVE MY SLOWNESS MY FRIENDS. OLD AGE, IT SEEMS, WILL NOT BE DENIED.

TAKE YER TIME, PAIL.

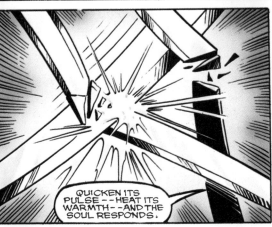

QUICKEN ITS PULSE -- HEAT ITS WARMTH -- AND THE SOUL RESPONDS.

TAKE MY HAND, FATHER...

I WILL HELP YOU.

ONLY BY PURIFYING MY SOUL -- BY THE SPILLING OF OTHERS' BLOOD BY THE BLOOD LUST OF MY OWN --

-- WILL I BE WORTHY OF MY TRUST!

NOW, FOLLOW MY LAMP -- IT WILL BE A BEACON THROUGH THE DARKENED STREETS...

...AND BEYOND.

BLOOD IS PURITY. MORE INTEGRAL THAN THE SO-CALLED SOUL,

WENG SAYS WE MUST *HURRY*.

I'M COMIN', PIERCE...

SIR?

I AM CUT. SPILT BLOOD... THE EBBING OF THE *FORCE*...

...BUT WHY DON'T I FEEL RIGHT 'BOUT THIS? I CAN'T SHAKE IT.

...LEADS TO DEATH. *I WILL NOT HAVE IT!*

AWW, YER GETTIN' PARANOID, FURY...

...THERE AIN'T NOTHIN' TO WORRY 'BOUT-- 'CEPT GETTIN' *KILLED*.

TRUST WENG, MR. PIERCE. HE HAS FOUND *HYDRA'S* LAIR. HE WILL NOT FAIL. DO NOT SHARE IN NICHOLAS'S *CYNICISM*.

A *FATHER'S FAITH* IS A TOUCHIN' THING, PAL.

BUT I GOTTA *HAND* IT TO YOU, WENG. YER CERTAINLY TAKIN' US ON THE *SCENIC ROUTE*.

I DON'T KNOW WHAT'S *WORSE*... FACIN' *HYDRA* OR SMELLIN' THAT SEWER. IT'S GETTIN' KINDA *RIPE* 'ROUND HERE.

IT IS THE ONLY WAY.

THIS IS THE LIFE! *HYDRA* BETTER WATCH OUT FOR ALEXANDER GOODWIN PIERCE!

I'M SURE THEY'RE TREMBLING.

CUT THE CRAP, BOYS, I THINK WE'RE *THERE*.

THE ONES YOU SEEK LIE *BELOW*.

THIS *TUNNEL* SMELLS WORSE THAN THE *SEWER.* YOU SURE THESE *HYDRA* GOONS OF YOURS ARE DOWN THERE?

COULD BE, MacKENZIE. THEY'RE JUST THE *TYPES* TO HANG OUT IN THE GUTTER.

I THINK MAC'S JUST AFRAID OF THE *DARK,* COLONEL.

VERY FUNNY, ALLEN.

I CAN'T WAIT TO GET MY HANDS ON SITWELL FOR GETTING ME INTO THIS.

SAVE YOUR AGGRESSION. YOU MAY BETTER DIRECT IT TOWARD THOSE WITHIN.

YOU SAID IT! FIRST, *HYDRA,* THEN THE *SHIELD* TURNCOATS.

LET'S GET THIS *OVER* WITH, GUYS.

NOW YOU ENTER, COLONEL.

NO. I'LL BRING UP THE *REAR.*

I'M OVERSEEIN' THIS DEAL, BUDDY BOY. YOUR *OLD MAN'S* HELPIN' ME! SO *I* GIVE THE ORDERS! NOW GET YOUR LANTERN INSIDE!

WHOA. DON'T KNOW WHAT I WOULDA DONE IF THE BIG GUY SAID *NO.* WHAT DID PAIL *FEED* HIM AS A KID?

BUT I CARRY THE LIGHT. YOU MAY BECOME LOST.

AND...

THEY HAVE ENTERED OUR OUTER PERIMETER?

YES, MADAME HYDRA. EXACTLY ON SCHEDULE.

THEY HAVE INFILTRATED THE *HYDRA* BASE?

YES, DEAR NICHOLAS IS SO *PREDICTABLE*. HE'S OFF TO SAVE THE WORLD AGAIN.

POOR CONFUSED FOOL. AH WELL, AFTER ALL THIS TIME, THE *END-GAME* BEGINS.

GAMES. ALWAYS GAMES. ISN'T THIS SO MUCH MORE?

LIFE IS A *GAME*, BELOVED. IF IT WERE NOT SO--

"-- THERE'D BE NO POINT TO *LIVING*."

SHALL I *ACTIVATE*, MADAME?

NO. LET THEM COME FURTHER IN. LET THEIR CONFIDENCE GROW.

IT IS SUCH A *FRAGILE* THING, CONFIDENCE ...

"...ONCE SHATTERED, ITS LOSS IS OFTEN IRREVOCABLE."

EVERYONE IN UNIFORM? GOOD.

IT IS INDEED.

WENG, DO NOT GO TOO FAR AHEAD.

WE'VE ONLY THE ONE LIGHT, AND THE WAY IS DARK.

YES, FATHER, IT IS.

DUNNO. CAN'T SHAKE THIS FEELIN' THAT SOMETHIN' AIN'T RIGHT. LIKE THERE'S SOMETHIN'... BAD... BACK THERE IN THE DARK.

NOW, I SHOULD THINK. POOR WENG. SUCH AN INNOCENT, REALLY. BUT ALL INNOCENCE MUST WITHER BEFORE THE GAZE OF HYDRA.

IMPLANT ENGAGED.

eeeeeee

WENG!

FWOOSH!

NO! NOT BEHIND, YOU IDIOT! IN FRONT! IT WAS IN FRONT OF YOU ALL THE TIME!

AGGH

FZZZATT

OOHH.

BLAST SHOULDA *KILLED* YOU, YOU FILTHY *LOWLIFE!* GET AWAY FROM HIM!

FURY?

YOU ARE *NOT* TO DIE.

HYDRA PAYIN' YOU *GOOD MONEY,* FAT STUFF? ENOUGH TO KILL YOUR OWN *FATHER?*

DO NOT SPEAK OF MY FATHER, LITTLE MAN!

FKO

OOFF

I HAVE ALWAYS *LOVED* AND *HONORED* MY FATHER!

ALWAYS!

CHOP

YOU'RE A *NUTCASE*, TUBBO! YOU *KILLED* ALLEN, MAYBE PIERCE--AND PAIL! AND YOU TALK OF *HONOR*!?

DON'T MAKE ME SICK!

PUNT

NO!

AGGHHH

WHOOPE

YOU KILLED MY *MEN*, WENG! MEN WHO *TRUSTED* ME! I'M SICK OF PEOPLE DYING! *SICK* OF IT!

AND YOU CAUSED IT, YOU HYDRA SCUM!

H-HOW LONG WAS I OUT? ALLEN--PAIL--*DEAD*? HOW DID IT HAPPEN? HOW DID WE *LET* THIS HAPPEN? WE WERE IN CONTROL!!

...BUT THE COLONEL SEEMS TO BE HANDLING THE SITUATION-- ACTING LIKE A TRUE SOLDIER--

--NOW'S MY CHANCE TO *PROVE MYSELF.* I WAS *WASTED* AS A SLEEPER AGENT! THIS IS WHAT I WAS *MEANT* TO DO! FOR *ALLEN!* FOR *PAIL!*

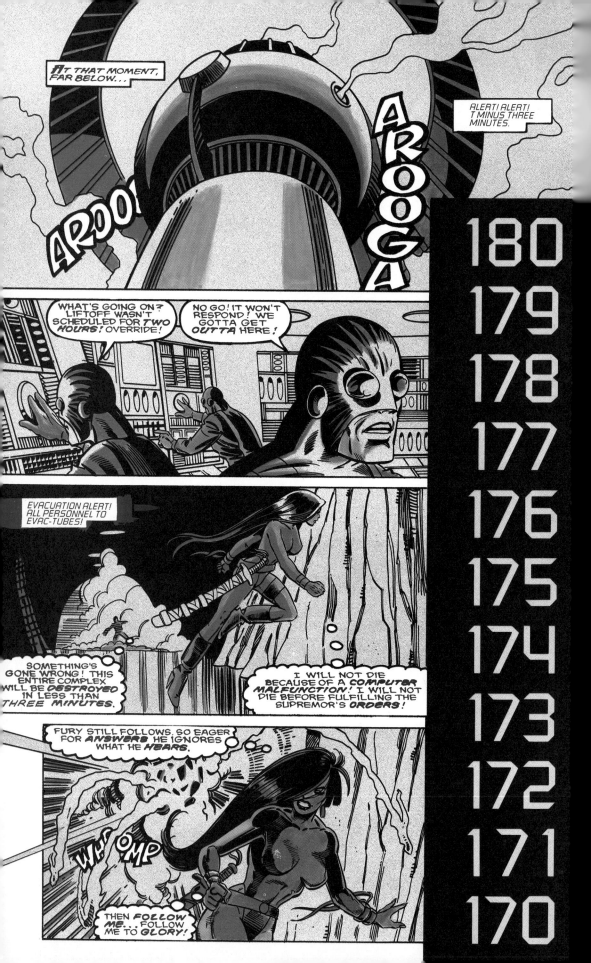

140
139
138
137
136
135
134
133
132
131
130
129
128
127

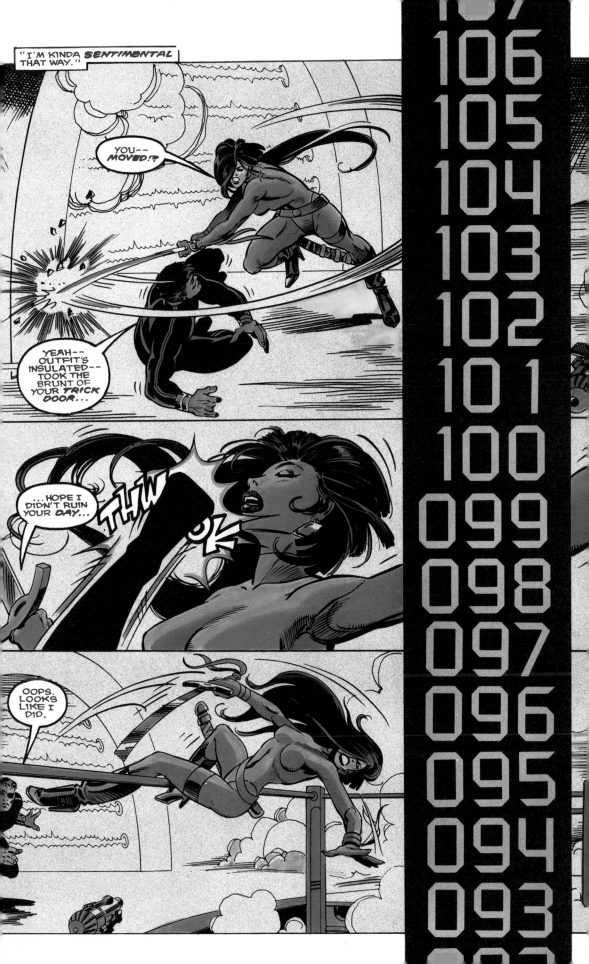

091
090
089
088
087
086
085
084
083
082
081
080
079
078
077

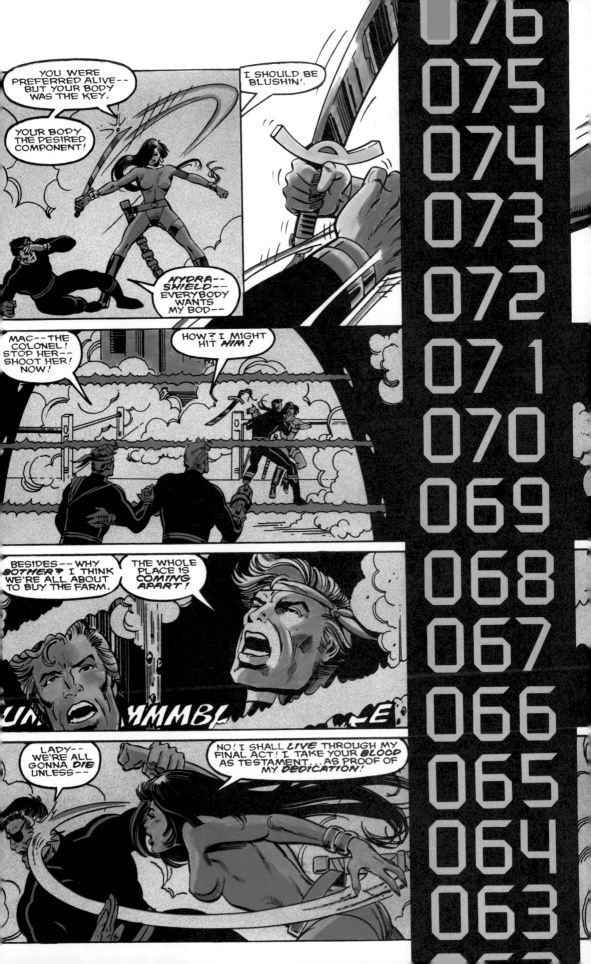

057
056
055
054
053
052
051
050
049
048
047
046
045
044
043

DEAD IS *DEAD!* SWEETS! NOTHIN' CHANGES THAT--NO FINAL ACT--NO REDEMPTION--NO *NOTHIN'* THAT'S THE SCARY THING ABOUT IT!

AN' I AIN'T READY TO *DIE* YET--SO LET'S GET *OUTTA* HERE!

NO! YOU MUST BE SENT AS *HYDRA* COMMANDS! HE WANTS YOUR *BLOOD*...IN PAYMENT FOR THE PAINS YOU HAVE INFLICTED ON THE SACRED BODY OF *HYDRA*.

I SAID *CAN IT!*

AW, GEEZ--DEBRIS FALLIN'. WE'RE IN *REAL* TROUBLE NOW!

INTO THE *SHIP*, FURY. YOUR DESTINY IS THERE!

LADY, LOOKS LIKE MY DESTINY IS TO GO *SPLAT* ON YOUR LAUNCH PAD.

COLONEL-- *JUMP!!*

GOOD IDEA, PIERCEY--

JUST BE THERE AN' *CATCH* US!

NO!

PIERCE, SOMETIMES-- *SOMETIMES*--YOU COME IN HANDY.

PIERCE, SOMETIMES-- SOMETIMES--YOU COME IN HANDY.

THE MISSILE LAUNCHES *WITHOUT* YOU--MY DEATH ACCOMPLISHES *NOTHING*--

YEAH, YOU'RE JUST GONNA BE PLAIN DEAD... LIKE EVERYBODY ELSE. IF YOU HAVE ANY SELF RESPECT, YOUR KING-SIZED *EGO* WILL GET US OUTTA HERE!

THE COUNTDOWN--

...REACHES ITS INEVITABLE CONCLUSION.

009
008
007
006
005
004
003
002
001
000

THERE IS *NO TIME*.

BULL! THERE'S ALWAYS TIME!

AND FURY?

WILL SOON BE HERE, AND ALL OUR FEARS WILL GIVE WAY TO *HOPE*.

THE GROUND-- *SHAKES!*

AND TO *LIFE*.

IGNITION!

NO! NOOOO!

"Someone is playin' games, manipulatin' us . . .
me . . . like puppets. And because of this sick,
perverted game too many people have died. There's
too much blood on my hands to turn back now."

chapter five: THE ASCENSION CALL

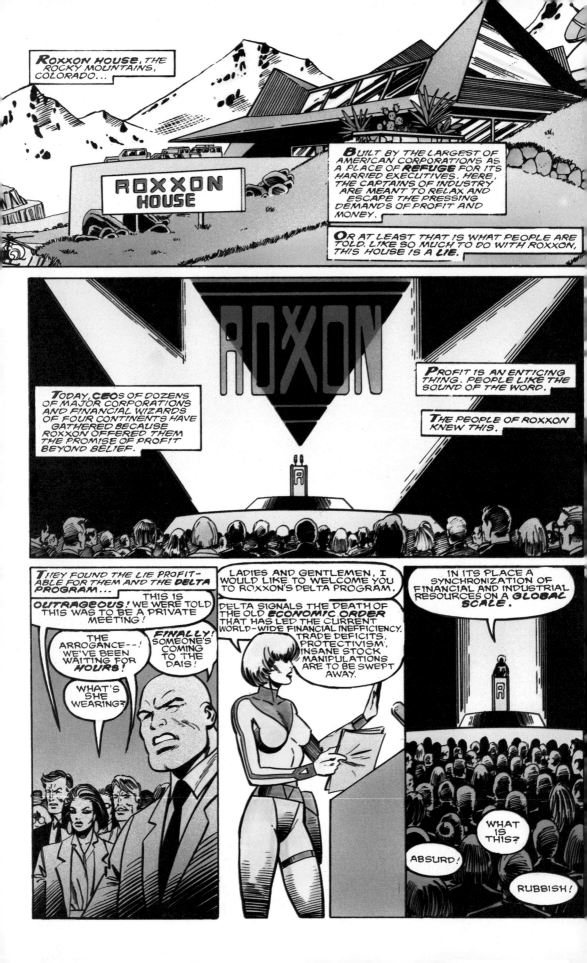

ROXXON HOUSE, THE ROCKY MOUNTAINS, COLORADO...

ROXXON HOUSE

BUILT BY THE LARGEST OF AMERICAN CORPORATIONS AS A PLACE OF *REFUGE* FOR ITS HARRIED EXECUTIVES. HERE, THE CAPTAINS OF INDUSTRY ARE MEANT TO RELAX AND ESCAPE THE PRESSING DEMANDS OF PROFIT AND MONEY.

OR AT LEAST THAT IS WHAT PEOPLE ARE TOLD. LIKE SO MUCH TO DO WITH ROXXON, THIS HOUSE IS A *LIE.*

TODAY, *CEO*S OF DOZENS OF MAJOR CORPORATIONS AND FINANCIAL WIZARDS OF FOUR CONTINENTS HAVE GATHERED BECAUSE ROXXON OFFERED THEM THE PROMISE OF PROFIT BEYOND BELIEF.

PROFIT IS AN ENTICING THING. PEOPLE LIKE THE SOUND OF THE WORD.

THE PEOPLE OF ROXXON KNEW THIS.

THEY FOUND THE LIE PROFIT-ABLE FOR THEM AND THE *DELTA* PROGRAM...

THIS IS *OUTRAGEOUS!* WE WERE TOLD THIS WAS TO BE A PRIVATE MEETING!

THE ARROGANCE--! WE'VE BEEN WAITING FOR *HOURS!*

FINALLY! SOMEONE'S COMING TO THE DAIS!

WHAT'S SHE WEARING?

LADIES AND GENTLEMEN, I WOULD LIKE TO WELCOME YOU TO ROXXON'S DELTA PROGRAM.

DELTA SIGNALS THE DEATH OF THE OLD *ECONOMIC ORDER* THAT HAS LED THE CURRENT WORLD-WIDE FINANCIAL INEFFICIENCY. TRADE DEFICITS, PROTECTIONISM, INSANE STOCK MANIPULATIONS ARE TO BE SWEPT AWAY.

IN ITS PLACE A SYNCHRONIZATION OF FINANCIAL AND INDUSTRIAL RESOURCES ON A *GLOBAL SCALE.*

WHAT IS THIS?

ABSURD!

RUBBISH!

"JIMMY, YOU'VE BECOME A REAL *DOWNER* LATELY."

QUARTERMAIN STILL *EXCELS* IN HIS TRIALS, JASPER?

"EXCELS" IS HARDLY THE WORD. HE'S DELTA'S *GREATEST ACHIEVEMENT*.

AND TO THINK, ROLLINS SOON, NONE OF THAT PERFECTION NEED EVER BE *LOST* AGAIN.

FATIGUE POISONS WITHIN *NORMAL RANGE*.

RESPIRATION UP 13.4%. CARDIOVASCULAR SCAN COMING IN.

YES, QUITE IMPRESSIVE. UNFORTUNATELY FOR *SOME* OF US--

-- THE CALL IS COMING A *BIT LATE!*

I'M *SORRY*, JACK. YOU KNOW THE *DECAY RATE* HAS ALWAYS BEEN UNPREDICTABLE.

AND SO I MUST *REGENERATE*-- BECOME MORE AND MORE LIKE *WOO* AND HIS ILK?

THEY *MUST* FIND FURY BEFORE THAT!

I WON'T ALLOW MYSELF TO BE *LOST!*

SLAM

AH, JACK, YOU MAY NOT HAVE ANY *CHOICE*.

DELTA.

BEHOLD, ENCODERS, YOUR HANDIWORK AND YOUR *MASTERPIECE!*

A BEING TRULY HUMAN, IN EVERY SENSE OF THE WORD, BORN AND BRED IN THE *WOMB* OF *DELTA.*

HE IS THE *HERALD* OF A NEW AGE. A RENAISSANCE FOR THE ELITE, WHO SHALL FOLLOW IN HIS FOOTSTEPS.

AND SOON THE *FINAL COMPONENT* WILL BE IN OUR HANDS. AS THE MASTER FORETOLD, THE TIMETABLE HAS *WORKED.*

TRULY, HE IS GENESIS REVISITED, BROTHERS! REGENERATION THROUGH DUPLICATION!

REPEATED LIFE IS *VALIDATED!*

HOLD... THE IMAGE ON THE SCREEN *SHIFTS.*

IT IS *THE MASTER!*

MY BRETHREN, THE TIME HAS COME. SOUND THE ASCENSION CALL. MAKE READY THE WAY.

THE CALL! THE CALL!

THE SAVIOR IS DELIVERED.

PERFECTION IS SAVED.

PATHETIC, SYNTHETIC THINGS. HOW EASILY WE *MANIPULATE* YOU.

IF FURY IS CAPTURED AT LAST, THINGS WILL MOVE *QUICKLY.* BUT FIRST, I MUST ATTEND...

...TO OUR *LATEST* RECRUITS.

ODD TO THINK THAT *THESE* CANDIDATES NEED NEVER FEAR REPEATED LIFE... THE LOSS OF *HEART* AND *SOUL.*

NOW, *STOP* IT, LAURA! IT IS A NEW *DAWN* DELTA, AND I CAN'T BEGRUDGE MY LOT IN LIFE NOW, CAN I?

COUNTESS, ISN'T THAT *LAURA BROWN* UP THERE ON THE BALCONY?

YOU'RE RIGHT, MIKE. THOUGH SHE'S THE *LAST* PERSON I EXPECTED TO SEE HERE... *IF* THIS IS DELTA.

MAYBE SHE CAN EXPLAIN SOME OF THIS.

LAURA, IT'S *VAL!* WHAT'S GOING ON? WE'VE BEEN IN BLIND TRANSPORT FOR DAYS.

WHERE ARE WE? THIS IS *NOT* STANDARD *SHIELD* PROCEDURE.

NO, IT IS NOT.

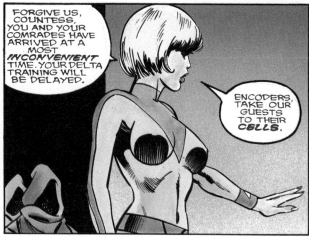

FORGIVE US, COUNTESS, YOU AND YOUR COMRADES HAVE ARRIVED AT A MOST *INCONVENIENT* TIME. YOUR DELTA TRAINING WILL BE DELAYED.

ENCODERS, TAKE OUR GUESTS TO THEIR *CELLS.*

WAIT ONE SECOND, LADY! HAVE YOU FORGOTTEN? I'M YOUR *SUPERIOR OFFICER*, YOU DON'T GIVE *ME* ORDERS!

COME, CANDIDATE, FOR YOUR TIME OF PREPARATION.

AND JUST WHO ARE *THESE* JOKERS?

WE ARE ENCODERS.

WE ARE TO PREPARE YOU FOR THE SACRAMENT OF ENCODING, THE FIRST STEP TO THE GIFT OF *REPEATED LIFE.*

REPEATED LIFE?

BUT FIRST YOU MUST CONTEMPLATE YOUR *PREVIOUS* EXISTENCE, YOUR SINS OF OMISSION AND COMMISSION...

GRIPS ARE SO TIGHT-- CAN'T BREAK FREE!

...SO PREPARE *HERE,* CANDIDATE, IN THE CELL OF *PENANCE.*

THIS IS JUST--

--DANDY!

I CAME HERE TO FIND OUT DELTA'S CONNECTION TO NICK'S DISAPPEARANCE... AND I END UP LORD KNOWS WHERE.

THE LORD HAS *LITTLE* TO DO WITH IT.

WHO?

THE NAME'S *NEVILLE*...

...AND THIS IS THE CLOSEST PLACE TO HELL ANYONE WILL FIND IN *THIS* LIFE, LADY.

SHIELDCENTRAL, NEW YORK.

THE COUNCIL REPORTS NICK WITHIN A FEW CLICKS OF *CAPTURE*.

LET'S HOPE THERE'S NO REPEAT OF THE HONG KONG FIASCO.

ROLLINS! AND YOU ONCE ACCUSED *ME* OF BLASPHEMY!

IF THE COUNCIL SAYS THAT LOSS CAME WITHIN THE PARAMETERS OF *ACCEPTABLE LOSS*, THEN WE ARE NOT TO QUESTION THEM.

LEVEL - 737

LEVEL - 738

NOW, QUARTERMAIN'S STATUS?

*ESP*ER SQUAD REPORTS UNUSUAL FRENETIC *ALPHA WAVES* IN HIS *REM* STATE INDICATING DISTURBING DREAMS TYPICAL OF *FIRST GENERATION*... BUT WE FIND THE *INTENSITY* OF HIS REMARKABLE.

DO *YOU* STILL DREAM, WOO? OR IS THAT ANOTHER ABILITY WE LOSE AS WE DECAY AND ARE *REBORN?*

ROLLINS —

NO! NO! NOOOO!

CLAY!

WAIT HERE!

CLAY... WHAT'S WRONG? WE HEARD YOUR *CRIES.*

BURNING, DEAR LORD, I WAS *BURNING!*

THESE DREAMS WON'T GO AWAY, *JACK.*

ROLLINS WAS CORRECT, *JASPER*...

I BECAME A DELTITE SO *LONG AGO...*

...THAT I HAVEN'T EVEN A *MEMORY* OF WHAT A DREAM IS.

OR A *WISH.*

OR A *HOPE.*

AND FOR THAT I CAN'T EVEN *GRIEVE.*

FLAMES SO REAL, JACK, I COULD ALMOST *TOUCH* THEM. I FELT THE HEAT...THE PAIN...

AGAIN HE REMEMBERS HIS DEATH. HE'S SO *HUMAN!* I WAS LIKE HIM ONCE... YOUNG...VITAL...

I DON'T REMEMBER... I *USED* TO...BUT MY MEMORY IS FADING! LIKE WOO'S FADED! I DON'T WANT TO DECAY! DO YOU HEAR ME--

I *DON'T WANT TO DECAY!*

ROLLINS!

WHERE'S FURY, JASPER? DOESN'T THE COUNCIL KNOW HOW MUCH HE *MEANS* TO US? WHY ARE THEY TAKING SO LONG *FINDING* HIM? *WHY?*

ATTENTION, ALL PERSONNEL! PREPARE FOR SPHERE ARRIVAL 0100 HOURS.

YES! *YES!*

SO NICK AND THE INFINITY FORMULA ARE WITHIN *GRASP.*

CONGRATULATIONS, GENTLEMEN, IT APPEARS YOU ARE TO BE SPARED THE RAVAGES OF *MY* FATE.

YOU SAID YOUR LIFE IS STRIPPED AWAY, KATE. *WHERE?*

TO SOMEPLACE ELSE...

...*NO*...

TO SOME*ONE* ELSE. THEY'RE GIVING HER MY LIFE.

SHE IS BECOMING... ME. OR SOMETHING *LIKE* ME.

"I'VE NEVER *SEEN* HER, BUT I KNOW SHE EXISTS. AS I DECREASE, SHE INCREASES... ISN'T THAT HOW THE SAYING GOES, COUNTESS?"

"WHATEVER... I FEEL HER GROWING STRONGER EVERY DAY."

ATTENTION! SPHERE ARRIVAL MINUS 2.45 HOURS.

DISENGAGE HER FROM THE UMBILICUS, GENTLY. SHE'S *FRIGHTENED.*

THEY'RE *ERASING* ME AND —

SWEET HEAVEN— *KATE!*

NO! NO! DON'T MOVE *ME! DON'T* MOVE *MEEEE!!*

GLORIOUS, ISN'T IT?

SHINING GLOBES DROPPING OH SO SOFTLY, SO EFFORTLESSLY INTO THE NIGHT.

OFF TO COLLECT THE FAITHFUL...

...THE CHOSEN...

...THE WILLING...

...THE UNWILLING...

ALL OF THEM.

AND NICHOLAS WILL BE HERE?

WITHOUT A DOUBT. I'VE TOYED WITH HIM LONG ENOUGH.

ONE GAME ENDS, ANOTHER BEGINS.

ALWAYS YOU SPEAK OF GAMES. IT WORRIES THE COUNCIL.

OH, THE POMPOUS POPINJAYS. THEY FORGET I GAVE THEM EVERYTHING... AS I GAVE THEM ALL LIFE.

BUT ANOTHER TOPIC. DO YOU LIKE YOUR PRESENT FORM, MY DEAR?

AFTER TOMORROW, IT WILL BE YOURS FOREVER. WILL YOU MISS BREWING A NEW GENETIC CONCOCTION WHEN THE MOOD STRIKES?

WILL YOU YEARN FOR THE DAYS OF WEAVING PERSONALITY TAPES INTO NEW AND ELEGANT TAPESTRIES?

ONLY WE KNEW THAT JOY.

TO BE TRUTHFUL, BELOVED...NO ONE ENJOYED IT AS MUCH AS YOU.

ASTOUNDING. NO DELTITE, EVEN ROLLINS OR I, REMEMBERS THE ENCODING OR THE REBIRTH.

I WONDER IF THE COUNCIL TRULY KNOWS WHAT THEY HAVE CREATED IN CLAY?

THIS ISN'T ME! THESE AREN'T MY HANDS! THIS IS THE OTHER!

BORN OUT OF CHEMICALS...IN THE WOMB CHAMBER! A FAKE!

I *FEEL* LIKE CLAY QUARTERMAIN--BUT I'M *NOT*! HE BURNED!

CLAY, FOR HEAVEN'S SAKE, CONTROL YOURSELF!

AND *YOU'RE* IN ON IT! SWEET HEAVEN, YOU'RE *LIKE* ME! A FORGERY WHO *THINKS* HE'S A MAN.

WHY DID THEY DO THIS TO ME?

WHY COULDN'T THEY LET ME DIE!?

CLAY!

WHAT *ARE* WE, JASPER? WHAAAARGGH!

THE PLASMA CHARGE SHOULD HAVE HIM OUT FOR HOURS.

HE IS REMARKABLE!

NO, JASPER. HE IS *DANGEROUS*.

LONDON, ENGLAND.

A DARKLING GLOBE, CLOAKED AGAINST ALL PRYING EYES, SAILS SILENTLY OVERHEARD...

...RESTING FINALLY OVER THAT ANCIENT CITY'S *SHIELD* COMPLEX.

THEN, THE CALL IS SOUNDED.

...LIKE THE ECHO OF DISTANT BELLS...

...AND DELTA CALLS ITS CHILDREN HOME.

NEW JERSEY...

WHEN DO WE MOVE IN, GABE? I'M GETTIN' ANTSY.

THERE'S SOMETHIN' BIG COMIN' DOWN. CAN'T YOU FEEL IT IN THE AIR?

YES, I CAN.

BUT THEY MUST *THINK* WE'RE DEAD. I DON'T WANT TO DO ANYTHING YET THAT WOULD DISSUADE THEM OF THAT NOTION.

WE SEEK NOT YOUR DEATHS, HUMANS...

OOOHBOY.

WE ONLY WISH TO BE UNDISTURBED AT THE SACRED MOMENT!

AND NONE MAY STOP US!

OOOHH

WHOA

WELCOME, O' SAVIOR OF ETERNITY--

--YOUR TIME OF FULFILLMENT IS AT HAND.

BUDDY, I DON'T KNOW WHO THE HECK *YOU* ARE-- BUT I KNOW...

...YOU... ...OR ONE OF YOU, ANYWAY. DIDN'T I KILL YOU IN A SEWER BACK IN NEW YORK?

OH, COME ON, NICK...

...YOU KILLED AN EARLIER *GENERATION* OF ME...

...BUT WITH REPEATED LIFE, NO ONE REALLY DIES...

...WE SIMPLY FADE AWAY.

BUT THAT IS ALL TO CHANGE, SAVIOR.

THANKS BE TO YOU.

RISE AND SHINE, LADIES!

WE'RE GOING ON A LITTLE TRIP.

LIGHT DISORIENTING YOU, VAL? THE HOLDING CELLS HAVE THAT EFFECT ON PEOPLE.

JUST JOIN YOUR FELLOW CANDIDATES. WE HAVE A LOT OF BUSINESS EXECUTIVES, VAL...

...MAYBE YOU'LL FIND A *CATCH*.

HOLD IT, LAURA. I WANT TO KNOW *WHERE* WE'RE BEING TAKEN.

YOU'LL FIND OUT SOON ENOUGH.

AND PLEASE GET YOUR HAND OFF ME, BEFORE I TAKE IT OFF.

TOKYO, CAPITAL OF JAPAN.

*A*NOTHER SPHERE SENDS OUT THE CALL...

S.H.I.E.L.D.

...AND INTO ITS MAW THE ASCENDANTS ARE SWALLOWED.

THANKS TO *ME*, BUDDY BOY?

BECAUSE OF THE *INFINITY FORMULA* IN MY VEINS? THAT LITTLE ADDITIVE THAT'S SLOWED DOWN MY AGING FOR THE PAST FIFTY ODD YEARS?

HOW INTELLIGENT IS THE SAVIOR! HOW--

CAN THE HOLY HOSANAS, OKAY?

SO YOU HAVE SURMISED YOUR IMPORTANCE TO DELTA?

SHIELD AND *HYDRA* WANTED MY BODY... WOO AGIN' LIKE HE DID... IT ADDED UP.

YES, THE FORMULA WILL ADD *STABILITY* TO OUR RANKS.

I WAS REGENERATED BEFORE MY TIME... BEFORE MY PREVIOUS LIFE HAD DECAYED SUFFICIENTLY... TO REVEAL OUR NEED TO YOU.

PRETTY POOR WAY TO TREAT A PERSON.

A LIFE SHOULD MEAN *MORE* THAN THAT. PEOPLE AREN'T XEROXES TO BE DUPLICATED JUST FOR A DEMONSTRATION.

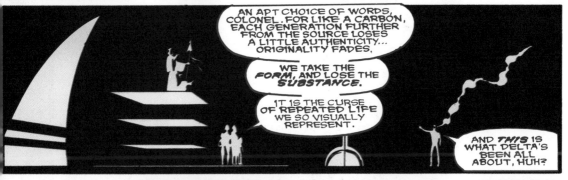

AN APT CHOICE OF WORDS, COLONEL. FOR LIKE A CARBON, EACH GENERATION FURTHER FROM THE SOURCE LOSES A LITTLE AUTHENTICITY... ORIGINALITY FADES.

WE TAKE THE *FORM*, AND LOSE THE *SUBSTANCE*.

IT IS THE CURSE OF REPEATED LIFE WE SO VISUALLY REPRESENT.

AND *THIS* IS WHAT DELTA'S BEEN ALL ABOUT, HUH?

YES! FOR WE ARE TO BRING *STRUCTURE* AND *ORDER* TO A WORLD OF CHAOS!

BEHOLD NOW YOUR PEOPLE.

THROUGH YOU WE WILL ACHIEVE A WORLD OF HARMONY AND REGULATION.

THEN, FROM THE EXPECTANT CROWD OF THOUSANDS COMES A SOUND...

...A CHANT PERHAPS, A MANTRA OR, BETTER STILL, A PRAYER THAT ECHOES THROUGH THE VAST COMPLEX.

FOR THIS IS THE DAY THEY WERE PROMISED...

...BY THE MAN WHO SITS...ABOVE.

A MAN WHO GAVE THEM LIFE AND PURPOSE...

AND IF THEY PARTAKE NONE OF THE SPOILS OF THIS DAY, IF IT IS ALL FOR THE ELITE, THE ENCODERS ARE STILL SATISFIED AND AT PEACE.

FOR IN THEM THERE IS NO DESIRE FOR UNIQUENESS, NO YEARNING FOR A PAST AND FADING LIFE. FOR THERE ARE NO MEMORIES TO CLING TO. NO HUMANITY TO MOURN.

THE ENCODERS HAVE THEIR FAITH, AND THAT IS ENOUGH.

FOR THE MAN TOLD THEM SO.

I DON'T UNDERSTAND! THE SUPREME HYDRA PROMISED ME *GLORIES UNTOLD* IF I DELIVERED FURY-- EITHER IN HONG KONG OR HERE!

YET, HE IS NOT TO BE SEEN! ONLY THESE FEEBLE PRIESTS WHO *WORSHIP* FURY AS IF HE WERE A GOD.

LADY, DON'T YOU SEE?

TO *THEM*, HE IS A GOD.

FOR TOO LONG THEY HAVE SUFFERED A CRUEL PUNISHMENT FOR THE DELTA SACRIFICE.

A LIFESPAN OF A FEW SHORT WEEKS BEFORE THE RUINATION OF AGE FORCES HOLY REGENERATION. AND WITH THAT, THE INEVITABLE LOSS OF SELF THE ELITE HOLD SO DEAR.

REMEMBER THE FIRST DELTITES WE ENCODED SO LONG AGO. NOW THEY ARE FADED... LITTLE MORE THAN WE, THEIR HUMBLE SERVANTS. ANGELS FALLEN FROM ON HIGH.

IS THAT WHAT YOU'RE AFRAID OF, KID?

IT'S WHAT WE ALL FEAR.

AND BY THE WAY, I'M NOT ANY XEROX... I'M ME. AS HUMAN AS YOU ARE.

I KNOW. THAT'S WHAT SCARES ME.

AND NOW, BRETHREN, WITH THE DELIVERANCE OF THE SAVIOR...

...THE GIFT OF REPEATED LIFE BECOMES THE SACRAMENT OF ENDURING LIFE!

SIR...ALL THIS... SINCE NEW YORK... JUST TO GET YOU?

YEAH, PIERCE.

THE WHOLE BLOODY MESS.

MELBOURNE, AUSTRALIA...

...AS IN MANY PLACES ACROSS THE FACE OF THE EARTH...

...THOSE CALLED THE ELITE AND THOSE CHOSEN FOR THAT SINGULAR HONOR...

...ARE CALLED HOME.

SHIELD-CENTRAL. JACK ROLLINS' PRIVATE QUARTERS.

SOON I'LL BE LIKE I WAS.

I WON'T HAVE LOST MUCH... SENSE OF TOUCH... A FEW MEMORIES MAYBE...

YEAH... NOT MUCH!

SMASH

I ONLY WANTED TO SERVE THE COLONEL... AND SHIELD.

... I NEVER ASKED FOR THIS.

I ONLY WANT TO LIVE... IS THAT SO WRONG?

NEW JERSEY.

GABE-- GET YOUR GUN!

I'M TRYING!

AH... BEHOLD, HEATHEN.

BEHOLD THE WONDERS OF DELTA!

SWEET MOTHER A' MERCY!

DELTA COMPLEX. ROXXON.

GOOD LORD! WHAT IS THIS PLACE? IT'S *IMMENSE.*

COUNTESS, THERE MUST BE *HUNDREDS* OF PEOPLE HERE!

MANY TIMES MORE THAN THAT, KATE...

...ALL GATHERED FOR THE FINAL MOMENT.

SHIELD CENTRAL.

IS EVERYONE ASSEMBLED, JIMMY?

ALL HAVE TAKEN THEIR PREARRANGED STATIONS...

...AWAITING THE FINAL MOMENT.

YES! YES!

LAURA!

SOME SORT OF TRACTOR BEAM! CAN'T RESIST IT!

COUNTESS... IT'S PULLING ME!

WHY, THIS IS QUITE REMARKABLE--

--WOULDN'T YOU AGREE?

IT IS FINISHED!

HEY-- EASY!

WHOA!

GABE...IT'S FLYIN'AWAY...

--AND ROXXON'S GONE DEAD!

THAT'S NOT ALL--TAKE A LOOK AT OUR FRIEND!

THE PLAN REACHES FRUITION...

...BUT SOME MUST EVER WITHER ON THE VINE! PARADISE IS NOT FOR ALL!

YES, I SUFFER GLADLY EXCOMMUNICATION...

...KNOWING MY BRETHEN CARRY ON...

...FOR ARE WE NOT ALL ONE?

GABE?

YO?

WHAT DO WE DO NOW?

SEARCH ME.

THE SPHERES ALL RETURN TO DOCK, EXACTLY ON SCHEDULE. AND WITH THEM, THE SEEDS OF THE FUTURE.

SOON, THE *INFINITY FORMULA* WILL BE SYNTHESIZED AS WE SO LONG PLANNED, EVERYTHING IS FALLING INTO PLACE.

WHY THEN DO I FEEL SO UNEASY?

PERHAPS YOU FEAR SUCCESS. A COMMON *HUMAN* TRAIT.

TRAITS AGAIN! YOU'VE BEEN IN COMMUNE WITH THE *PROGENITORS* I TAKE IT.

I'M ALWAYS IN COMMUNE WITH THEM...IN MY HEAD, BUT YES, I PLAYED THE PERSONA TAPES.

AS ALWAYS A RAMBUNCTIOUS, ARGUMENTATIVE LOT.

PERHAPS YOU DEPEND ON THEM... TOO MUCH. THEIR CHAOTIC TRAITS WERE NEVER WEEDED OUT.

FROM THAT FIRST DAY WHEN I STUMBLED ONTO THEM... AND HARVESTED THEIR MOST *USEFUL* FACETS...

...THEY HAVE BEEN ME, THEY ARE MY *SOUL*.

AND IF NOT FOR THEM, WE WOULD NOT HAVE SUCCEEDED THIS DAY. REMEMBER THAT, MY LOVE.

"You made my whole life a lie . . . killed my people . . .
my friends . . . you took what was good an' noble
and made it something twisted and rotten. And
you're gonna pay!"

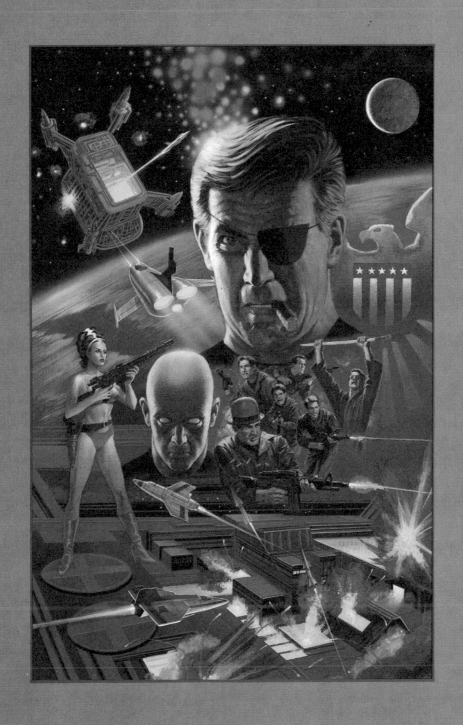

chapter six: *LIGHT OF TRUTH*

CREATOR, IT IS FINISHED. OUR LONG JOURNEY IS COMPLETE.

THE ETERNITY FORMULA HAS BEEN ISOLATED. ITS GENETIC MATRIX THOROUGHLY ANALYZED.

THE LIFE-PROLONGING PROPERTIES THAT HAS ALLOWED NICHOLAS FURY TO LIVE UNAGING FOR SO LONG CAN NOW BE TRANSFERRED TO THE ELITE.

REPEATED LIFE HAS BEEN WASHED AWAY BY THE COMING OF THE SAVIOR. IT IS A JOYOUS DAY.

OF COURSE, MASTER ENCODER. I AM TOUCHED BY YOUR RAPTURE.

BUT BEFORE YOU BEGIN SINGING PSALMS, ENGAGE THE TRANSMUTATION PROCESS.

...THE FIRST TRANSFER WILL BE *MINE*.

YOU?

BELOVED?

THIS IS...UNEXPECTED. IT HAS ALWAYS BEEN PART OF THE DESIGN THAT OUR MOST GENETICALLY PERFECT DELTITE BE THE *FIRST* TO RECEIVE THE FORMULA.

CLAY QUARTERMAIN IS THE VANGUARD OF OUR FUTURE. HE MUST BE PRESERVED BEFORE DECAY SETS IN.

MY DEAR, YOU YOURSELF TOLD ME CLAY IS OFF BROODING...

...AND, IT IS TIME YOU LEARNED, PLANS DO CHANGE.

BUT NOT US! IF YOU *ALTER* THE PLAN... YOU *RUIN* THE SYMMETRY OF THE FUTURE.

WE WILL ENTER THE CYCLE OF CHAOS AND UNPREDICTABILITY! IS THAT NOT WHAT WE SEEK TO ESCAPE?

IS NOT ORDER...PRECIOUS, STRUCTURED ORDER...THE VERY HEART OF THE PLAN?

...STRIKE!!

GIVE ME THAT, CHILD!

LIKE-- OWWW!

HYDRA! WAY TO GO!

SO YOU ACT LIKE A WARRIOR AGAIN, EH, ALEXANDER GOODWIN PIERCE?

THE CALL TO BATTLE STILL STIRS YOU?

GOOD. I FEARED YOU LOST IT.

SOUND THE ALARM! A CANDIDATE ATTACKS THE ELITE!

ENCODER, I'VE HAD ENOUGH OF YOU!

POW

HOLY-- THEY'RE PULLING IT OFF!

WAY TO GO!

COME ON-- LET'S MOVE!

COUNTESS?

LETHARGY WAS OUR GREATEST ENEMY, KATE.

LOOKS LIKE ALL WE NEEDED WAS A LOONEY TO SHOW US THE WAY! COME ON!

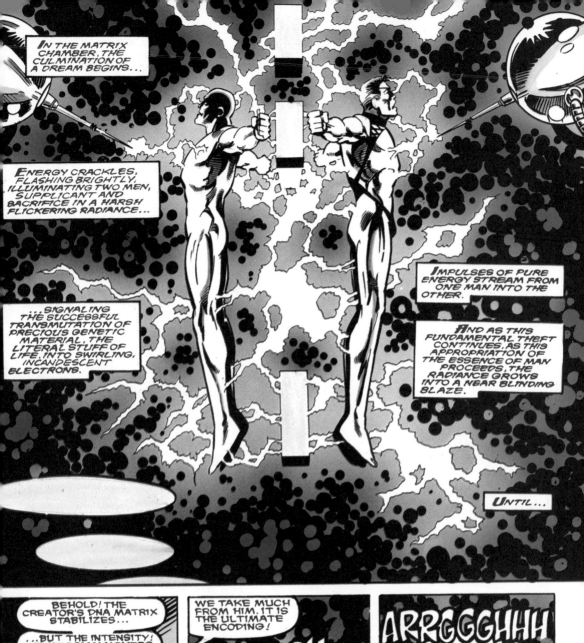

IN THE MATRIX CHAMBER, THE CULMINATION OF A DREAM BEGINS...

ENERGY CRACKLES, FLASHING BRIGHTLY, ILLUMINATING TWO MEN, SUPPLICANT AND SACRIFICE IN A HARSH FLICKERING RADIANCE...

...SIGNALING THE SUCCESSFUL TRANSMUTATION OF PRECIOUS GENETIC MATERIAL, THE LITERAL STUFF OF LIFE, INTO SWIRLING, INCANDESCENT ELECTRONS.

IMPULSES OF PURE ENERGY STREAM FROM ONE MAN INTO THE OTHER.

AND AS THIS FUNDAMENTAL THEFT CONTINUES, AS THIS APPROPRIATION OF THE ESSENCE OF MAN PROCEEDS, THE RADIANCE GROWS INTO A NEAR BLINDING BLAZE.

UNTIL...

BEHOLD! THE CREATOR'S DNA MATRIX STABILIZES...

...BUT THE INTENSITY! THE MESSIAH HOVERS NEAR DEATH!

THE SACRED FORMULA IS BONDED FIRMLY TO HIS MORTAL FRAME.

WE TAKE MUCH FROM HIM. IT IS THE ULTIMATE ENCODING!

ARRGGGHHH

ARRGGGHHH

ENCODER-- BY ALL YOU HOLD HOLY-- STOP!

THE HOLDING CELL...

WE HAVE VANQUISHED OUR CAPTORS, PIERCE. THEIR BLOOD IS OURS.

NOW, WE MUST ATTACK OUR OPPRESSORS... LIKE TRUE WARRIORS BORN.

KEEP BABBLING, SWEET-HEART.

HOLD IT, HYDRA!

THE DAY YOU ISSUE ORDERS TO *SHIELD* AGENTS IS THE DAY HELL FREEZES OVER.

GET HER GUN, PIERCE.

WITH PLEASURE, COUNTESS.

YOU WILL *PAY* FOR THIS INDIGNITY... "COUNTESS".

I'LL LOSE SLEEP, LADY.

BUT NOW...

...LET'S GET OUT OF THIS PIT!

NO... YOU DO NOT UNDERSTAND...

...AND SO YOU SIN...

...BUT, OH!

WE WERE TO GIVE YOU SUCH A GIFT!

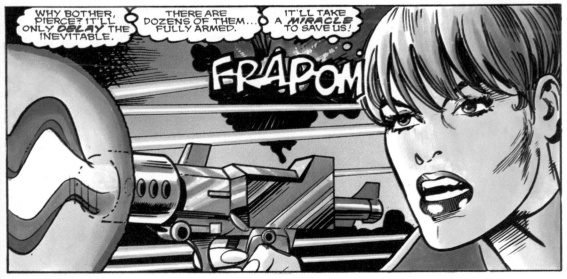

BELOW...

DEAR LORD-- HE RELEASED THE CORE!

THE CORE!

HE TOOK THE BRUNT OF THE POWER SURGE...

...HE'S BADLY BURNED.

JACK, LEND ME A HAND.

WE'VE GOT TO GET OUT OF HERE...WARN THE OTHERS...

...BEFORE IT'S TOO LATE.

YEAH "FRIEND"...

...YOU USED ME ALL RIGHT. PLAYED ME LIKE A PRIZE CHUMP ALL THESE YEARS--

--YEARS!

...KILLED MY PEOPLE... MY FRIENDS...

YOU MADE MY WHOLE LIFE A LIE...

YOU TOOK WHAT WAS GOOD AN' NOBLE AND MADE IT SOMETHING TWISTED AND ROTTEN.

SMASH

AND YOU'RE GONNA PAY!

TEMPER, COLONEL.

MAYBE I CREATED AN EFFICIENT ORGANIZATION FOR YOU--

--AND MAYBE YOU LAUGHED AND MADE IT YOUR TOOL--

--BUT YOU NEVER UNDERSTOOD IT. YOU COULDN'T!

SWOK!

YOU THINK YOU'VE COME SO FAR, BUDDY!

BUT ALL YOUR LIFE ALL YOU'VE DONE IS FOLLOW YOUR ORIGINAL PROGRAMMING. YOU "MAINTAIN" THINGS.

YOU HAVEN'T MOVED FAR FROM THE BILGE TUBES NO MATTER *WHAT* YOU THINK.

NO--LIGHT HEADED... CAN'T AFFORD... WHY NOW?

NICHOLAS, PERHAPS YOUR MIND HAS GROWN FEEBLE FROM AGE.

THINK! YOU UNDERWENT THE TRANSMUTATION! YOU NEARLY DIED...

...WHILE I WAS STRENGTHENED.

POOR DULLARD! YOU NEVER WERE A THINKER, WERE YOU, FURY? NO. YOU RELIED ON BRUTE STRENGTH TO SURVIVE. HOW ILL-EQUIPPED YOU TRULY WERE FOR THE ART OF SUBTERFUGE. AND HOW IT PROVES YOUR UNDOING.

YOUR OPPONENT IS YOUR GENETIC AND IN-TELLECTUAL SUPERIOR! AND HE HAS HURT YOU DEEPLY, FURY. IN YOUR SOUL!

IF A COLLECTION OF DATA BANKS CAN FEEL EMOTION, THEN I WOULD SAY ON THIS DAY I AM, OVERJOYED.

FOR, ALTHOUGH I AM DEAD, THROUGH HIS EYES, I WILL FINALLY SEE YOU VANQUISHED.

STRUCKER!

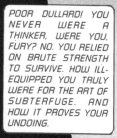

ONLY THE PERSONA TAPE OF YOUR LONG-DECEASED FOE, FURY. YET HE IS ONLY BUT A PART OF MY MIND--

--THERE ARE OTHERS!

WHATEVER IT WAS, IT'S STOPPED.

QUIET AS A GRAVE.

NICE CHOICE OF WORDS, PIERCE.

IS EVERYBODY THROUGH?

YOU'RE THE LAST, MA'AM.

PIERCE, WHAT'S KEEPING YOU? COME ON!

HOLY--

COUNTESS! BEHIND US... SOME SORT OF ENERGY FIELD... MOVING FAST.

WHAT COULD IT BE?

I HAVE A SUSPICION. AND IF I'M RIGHT, WE'RE IN DEEPER TROUBLE THAN I THOUGHT.

YOUR EXODUS HAS LED US TO A DEAD END, COUNTESS.

ALL THAT AWAITS US IS A BANK OF ELEVATORS. WHAT DO YOU PROPOSE WE DO NOW?

VAL! THE CREST ON THIS BUTTON-- I'VE SEEN IT BEFORE.

AT DELTA.

THEN, LET'S PRESS IT.

AND SEE WHERE IT TAKES US.

SECONDS AND MANY DECKS LATER...

LOOKS LIKE WE HIT THE JACKPOT.

WHAT IS *THIS*?

WELL, WELL. ALL MY PAWNS GATHERED AT LAST! SUCH SPIRIT... THEY DO THEIR ORGANIZATION PROUD.

I SHOULD ATTEMPT NOTHING, VALENTINA. MY ENCODERS HAVE YOU COVERED.

NICK!

WHAT HAVE YOU DONE TO HIM?

EASY, COUNTESS. THE COLONEL WOULDN'T WANT US TO DO ANYTHING RASH.

THE FOOLS! IT IS THEY WHO HAVE DESTROYED US. WE SHOULD HAVE GASSED THEM IMMEDIATELY.

TO LOSE NOW IS UNTHINKABLE! I WILL NOT FACE NON-EXISTENCE BECAUSE OF THESE NON-ARYANS.

ALL IS UNDONE, BELOVED. YET YOU LAUGH?

WHO WOULD NOT? WE STROVE FOR ORDER AND ALL IS ANARCHY!

YEARS OF PLANNING, BREEDING, REPLICATING... ALL UNDONE BY THE *ONE* DELTITE OF WHOM WE WERE SO PROUD.

WE MADE HIM TOO WELL! HE HAD HUMAN FEELINGS THAT REFUSED OUR PLAN. WE ARE DESTROYED BY A THING WE FEARED AND REJECTED: INDIVIDUALITY.

IT HAS STRUCK US LIKE A VIPER!

THE HUMAN SPIRIT SEEMINGLY CANNOT BE VANQUISHED!

PIECE OF DEBRIS... JUST GOTTA REACH...

WE SOUGHT TO ELIMINATE IT. BUT IT REFUSED TO DIE IN CLAY AND SO THIS GAME ENDS.

YOU HAVE THE NERVE TO TALK OF MASS MURDER AS A *DIVERSION!?*

SIMPLY PUT... YES.

BUT, NOW WITH THE INFINITY FORMULA IN ME, I MUST LEAVE. I HAVE YEARS TO EXPERIMENT ON THIS THING CALLED LIFE.

AS *SHIELD* DIES... A NEW BEGINNING IS OPEN TO ME. NEW PEOPLE BEG TO BE EXPLORED. AND THANKS TO YOU, NICK-- I SHALL *UNDERSTAND* THEM... MOLD THEM... *CONTROL* THEM.

NO!

YOU AIN'T HURTIN' ANYONE EVER AGAIN! *UNDERSTAND?*

VIPPP

ARGGH!

YOU USED PEOPLE... ROBBED 'EM OF DIGNITY... OF *LIFE!* AN' NOW YOU PAY THE PRICE!

YOU WANTED A STAGNANT WORLD OF AUTOMATED EMPTY PEOPLE?

WELL, YOU *LOST!* 'CAUSE CLAY QUARTERMAIN HAD TOO MUCH IN 'IM FOR YOU TO SNUFF IT OUT!

AND WHAT HE DID, HE DID FOR *ALL* OF US! 'CAUSE WE'RE GOIN' TO DIE *FREE!*

AND, NICHOLAS...

I... WHAT I DO, I DO FOR ME!

DEAR LORD—HE CAN'T GET AWAY!

DELTITES, IS *THIS* WHAT YOUR BLASTED PLAN OF PEACE AND ORDER HAS COME TO?

REDUCED TO ASHES BY THE EGO OF A MEGLOMANIAC!

BE AT EASE, CLAY QUARTERMAIN.

BELOVED, I HAVE HEARD MUCH THIS NIGHT...TO MY PAIN AND SORROW.

YOU HAVE BETRAYED US ALL, THOSE YOU BRED TO SERVE AND LOVE YOU.

YOU HAVE DEMONSTRATED THAT WE EXIST FOR NOTHING NOW, FOR YOU HAVE BECOME LIKE THEM: INWARD AND SELFISH.

WE WERE MERELY TOYS FOR YOU, TO BE DISCARDED AT DAY'S END.

NICK FURY SAID YOU CANNOT USE PEOPLE.

HE WAS RIGHT.

ENCODERS, EXCOMMUNICATE THE FALSE GOD!

DARLING, DON'T BE RASH. COME WITH...

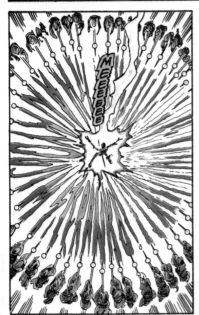

MEEEEE

THEY KILLED HIM—

NICK! ARE YOU ALL RIGHT?!

YEAH, VAL. I'M OKAY. LONG TIME NO SEE, HUH?

BUT WE DON'T HAVE MUCH TIME.

THE CORE?

TAKE 'EM ALL TO THE *LIFE CELLS*, VAL' BLAST *EVERYBODY* BACK TO EARTH.

AND DON'T LOSE ANY OF THOSE CORPORATE JOES, I DON'T WANT US GETTIN' *SUED*.

WHAT ABOUT YOU?

I'LL BE THERE SOON.

RIGHT NOW, I'VE GOT *BUSINESS* TO ATTEND TO.

I FOUND OUT A LOT TODAY. LIKE WHO YOU ARE.

YOU'RE MY FRIENDS... VICTIMS OF SOME MADMAN'S SCHEME.

COME WITH US. MAYBE WE CAN HELP YOU.

HOW, COLONEL? WE WERE EXPOSED TO *LETHAL* RAD LEVELS.

MAYBE NOW, AT THE END, OUR *TRUE* PERSONALITIES ARE COMING TO THE FORE. I CAN THINK CLEARLY NOW.

AS CLAY SAID, WE'VE DIED ALREADY. IT IS ENOUGH.

WELCOME BACK, JASP.

DON'T MOURN US, NICK. WE'RE ARTIFICES. THINGS. BUT AT LEAST ALLOW US THE DIGNITY OF DYING AS *MEN* THIS TIME.

COLONEL, I ONLY WANTED TO BE A GOOD *SHIELD* AGENT...

...TO SERVE YOU.

I... KNOW, JACKIE...

I'M SORRY... MORE SORRY THAN I CAN SAY.

DON'T DO THIS... THERE'S STILL TIME.

LEAVE US, NICK. SAVE *YOURSELF*.

FOR IT ENDS HERE.

COLONEL... I *THINK*... I *DREAM*... ISN'T THAT WHAT MAKES A PERSON?

I DIDN'T ASK FOR THIS!

REMEMBER *US!*

COME, JACK. I BROUGHT YOU TO DELTA...

...LET ME ATONE AND BRING YOU TO FINAL PEACE.

JACK... JIMMY...

A SILENT MOMENT.

PERHAPS A PRAYER.

THEN...

OH. I FORGOT ABOUT *YOU.*

FEAR NOT. WE ARE DONE. OUR WISH FOR A WORLD OF STRUCTURE AND COHESION IS DEAD.

OUR PLAN WOULD HAVE BROUGHT PEACE. IS THAT SO WRONG?

AT THE PRICE OF *HUMANITY?* YOU BET!

THEN NOTHING IS LEFT NOW BUT PURGATORY.

GO NOW... TO YOUR WORLD OF CHAOS AND EGO. AND BE WELCOME TO IT.

"AS *WE* WELCOME OUR END."

GOTTA MOVE... JUST HOPE VAL GOT EVERYONE OFF.

THEY LEFT A SINGLE CELL FOR *ME!* GOOD GIRL!

JUST HOPE I CLEAR THE SHIP *BEFORE* SHE BLOWS.

A SILENT LAUNCH...

...AS THE GREAT SHIP YAWS OUT OF ORBIT...

...A SUDDEN RADIANCE CONSUMES ALL...

...AS SEVERAL MILLION TONS OF SPACECRAFT JOINS THE ETERNAL ETHER.

AND...

STEADY! DO YOU HAVE HIM YET?

YEP! I'M HANDLIN' HIM WITH KID GLOVES.

GABE! DUM DUM, YOU OLD WALRUS!

IF I WAS SENTIMENTAL, I'D HUG THE *BOTH* OF YOU!

HOW'D YOU FIND US?

EASIEST PART OF THIS WHOLE AFFAIR! WE SIMPLY FOLLOWED THE TRAJECTORY OF THE SPHERES BACK INTO SPACE.

BUT ENOUGH OF THAT! WELCOME HOME, OLD BUDDY!

IT'S ALL OVER.

NO, GABE.

NOT YET.

WEEKS LATER...

"UNITED NATIONS RESOLUTION 487, ...AND THUS, IN ACCORDANCE WITH THE EVIDENCE AND THE RECOMMENDATIONS OF COLONEL NICHOLAS FURY, IT IS DECIDED THAT SHIELD, HAVING PROVED TO BE A MAJOR INTERNATIONAL SECURITY RISK...

"...BE IMMEDIATELY DISBANDED. ALL OPERATIONS SHALL BE TERMINATED, INSTALLATIONS NEUTRALIZED.

"ALL REMAINING PERSONNEL ARE TO BE DEBRIEFED AND DISCHARGED."

NICK...WE HAVE TO GO.

I KNOW.

I WAS JUST THINKIN' OF ALL OF 'EM... FOR A WHILE.

...REMEMBERIN'...

BUT YOU'RE RIGHT.

IT'S TIME, TROOPS.

SOMEBODY HIT THE LIGHTS.

AND DARKNESS FALLS ACROSS A PLACE CALLED SHIELD.

published by
THE MARVEL ENTERTAINMENT GROUP
387 Park Avenue South
New York, NY 10016
ISBN #: 0-87135-554-X